W9-AHG-319

A BAD CASE

AND OTHER ADVENTURES
OF DISTURBED MINDS

What links Clorinda to the mysterious disappearance of her new friend Theresa, in broad daylight, on the streets of New York? What is the true relationship between high-born, nine-year-old Elise von Alpenberg and her sinister guardian, Kepler von Thul? Why does young Marthe's uneasy interview with the notorious spy, Anthony Blunt, stir up suspicions of complicity against her boss, the Establishment socialite Barbara? And who is the *true* Fourth Man? And what connects Barbara to Constance Bryde, an unfaithful wife enmeshed in the cat-and-mouse surveillance operations of a divorce solicitor's enquiry agent? Or how will jilted mistress, Rhona, deliver a long-overdue comeuppance to her Significant Other, the supercilious on-screen Talking Head? And who, you may well wonder, is the next doomed subject of portraitist Deverell-Hewells's murderous thoughts? And, finally, can Nina discreetly maintain the façade that hides the eternal triangle of her complicated lovelife? These questions and more are answered in Eisner's third series of mordant case histories intimately documenting bizarre dramas triggered by the subclinical dependencies of disturbed minds.

Do I need to describe my wife when an artist greater than myself has captured her essence . . . It's a living likeness! For long ago she had reached that moment in the passage of a woman's life when, as it is said, the mirror no longer returns the expected consoling reflection and, therefore, must be turned to the wall.

Royal Portraitist Prof. Anthony Deverell-Hewells
Page 154, *Now You See It, Now You Don't.*

A BAD CASE

AND OTHER ADVENTURES
OF DISTURBED MINDS

CATHERINE
EISNER

SALT

CROMER

PUBLISHED BY SALT
12 Norwich Road, Cromer, Norfolk NR27 0AX

The right of Catherine Eisner to be identified as the author of this work has been asserted by her in accordance with Section 77 of the Copyright, Designs and Patents Act 1988.

First published by Salt Publishing, 2014

Printed in Great Britain by Clays Ltd, St Ives plc

Typeset in Paperback 9/12

ISBN 978 1 84471 962 4 paperback

1 3 5 7 9 8 6 4 2

'There is a fissure in my vision and madness will always rush through.'

ANAÏS NIN

CONTENTS

AN INTRODUCTION
TO . . .

. . . seven wayward individuals divided by unreason, yet united by their medical histories, which, as you'll observe, reveal a disregarded nutritional imbalance as the causative agent of their undoing.

A chemical brew indeed.

As legendary drug fiend, and self-confessed 'alchemist', **Keith Richards** remarked, 'I looked upon the body as a laboratory . . . I was intrigued by that . . . But all experiments must come to an end.'

Yet for some, as these cases demonstrate, the dependency cannot end.

In the case of **Anthony Blunt,** the spy who drank like a fish (*In Search of the Fourth Man*), his decades-long dependence on barbiturates (Seconal) was complicated by his alcoholism. Blunt would start drinking at 11 o'clock in the morning, and his alcoholism almost certainly inhibited the anaesthetic activity of his brain's barbiturate receptor sites. These co-existing counteractions would have significantly increased the anxiety neurosis that his chronic alcohol ingestion sustained.

Then consider the case of **Lewis Carroll** (*A Bad Case*). What are we to make of the tincture of opium he partook with his hosts at the country house tea party, and of his extreme, disproportionate reaction to the drug manifested in those strange episodes of sensory-perceptual distortions he experienced on that June afternoon in 1863? A faddish man, who ate only one frugal meal a day, Carroll was in consequence most likely to be deficient in dietary folates; a deficiency which a side dish of leafy vegetables such as spinach, lettuce and fresh greens would have corrected. This folate supplement is now known to be beneficial in metabolic dysfunctions related to psychoses resembling hallucinogenic drug-induced states.

Metabolic dysfunctions, we may guess, also figure prominently in *Darkly, More is Seen*, which relates the case of perfectionistic **Rhona 'Clingwrap'** whose own self-assessment admits to the low body weight of chronic undernourishment, witness arms 'as thin as a grasshopper's' (nor did she neglect to mention that her 'clothes hung off' her). It's clear that Rhona's co-existing confusional state is induced as much by the shock of her lover's rejection as by her eating disorder, a dissociative reaction manifested in the ensuing mood swings and stalking behaviour compounded by the distress that follows a romance that's soured.

Similarly, not unnaturally, given her predicament, **Theresa Ollivante** (*A Room to the End of Fall*) is a victim of severe vitamin deficiencies, due to her revulsion from the rancid stocks of survivalist carbohydrate supplements and bulgur wheat wafers that, latterly, were her principal source of nutrients. Theresa records her aversion to 'a dehydrated ham and egg omelet with a side order of instant white rice,' yet sees the wisdom of persisting with powdered eggs as an essential source of Vitamin D to counter the anaemia that sunlight deprivation would give rise to. Individuals deficient in Vitamin D complain of lightheadedness, vertigo, nausea, muscle weakness, and submission to fatigue, all symptoms and complications Theresa fought against doughtily when confined in her long-sought-after 'separate room'.

Of the portraitist, **Anthony Deverell-Hewells** (*Now You*

See It, Now You Don't), the least said the better, since his criminal meddling with the emetic properties of a scarce mineral, in alchemical experiments to determine their precise action upon his victim's gastrointestinal tract, may have turned his mind. But, since these chemical transmutations are the substance of Deverell-Hewells's confessional narrative, I direct you, the jury, to judge him only when you've heard him out.

And then there is **Nina** (*Private Ledger*), can we be certain that her propensity for drinking 'extra frozen margaritas in her PJs on the terrace', and post-coital absinthe in the afternoons, has not followed the pattern of Blunt's chronic alcohol ingestion and clouded her judgement by magnifying her neuroses to an agitation that sometimes makes her heedless of errors or blind to the consequences of racing thoughts unconstrained by guilt or remorse.

Which leaves **Constance Bryde** (*Inducement*) and her 'epicene' husband to be submitted to an initial diagnostic impression. Certainly, judged by their regular tipples, single malt whisky and eighty proof vodka make unsuitable bedfellows. Malnutrition, of course, is an attendant hazard of excessive alcohol ingestion, despite its theoretical calorific value. A dependence on coarser sweet foodstuffs (in Simon Bryde's case, Creamola rice custard further sweetened by Nannie) is associated with alcohol dependence, and explains the nursery-tea-faddiness of Constance's husband, rather than the infantilism she imputes to him. Alcohol dependence and malnutrition also induce sleep disorders by disrupting normal sleep patterns, a weakness Constance is tempted to exploit, and a circumstance that advances my thesis that nutritional imbalances can be seen as the triggers to the misadventures of disturbed minds documented here.

As – *reductio ad absurdum!* – the callow critic says of Oswald, the unfortunate juvenile lead in **Ibsen**'s *Ghosts*:

'Invent *Salvarsan* and Oswald's syphilis is cured; the problem of inherited syphilis disappears and Oswald just doesn't get a social disease. No disease, no problem. No problem, no play.'

Well. I regret that what remedies there may exist for the troubled minds we meet in these narratives will be found to be altogether untimely in their efficacy, and in consequence the problems that beset the protagonists remain and, hence, their dramas are played out on these pages by actors without any thought of a cure.

CATHERINE EISNER 2014

For further clinico-psychological observations on the characteristics and culture of these individuals, please consult the brief *Notes* in the final section of this book.

Filename: **Theresa Ollivante**
Classification: **Mistaken identity**

A ROOM TO THE END OF FALL

'The death sentence and the life sentence are equally immoral, but if I had to choose between the death penalty and imprisonment for life, I would certainly choose the second. To live anyhow is better than not at all.'
The Bet, by Anton Chekhov (1888).
A story of an incarceration.

Please note: To allay suspicions of editorial tampering (spelling, punctuation, usage, etc.), which for very sound reasons this American narrator maintains, her native US orthography in this account remains unchanged.

A ROOM TO THE END OF FALL

That the house had no flag should have first alerted me to a significant departure from the norm.

It's true the Stars and Stripes were seen to flutter above the neighboring stoops, but my gaze had been drawn to a pair of blue jays bobbing in the depths of a sweet gum tree as they fought for swollen seed pods.

Pinned to the trunk was a *Resist the Draft* handbill; the following Thursday had been declared a national Turn-in-Your-Draft-Card Day.

Shade trees overhung the length of the sidewalk; their leaves were flame red; it was mid-Fall.

Even then, I could have turned back, yet I stood there quite lost, musing on the day's chances that had led me to that spot.

I had a strange, uneasy sense that the moment was preordained; that all I had said and done that morning had been assigned to me in an unalterable series of steps toward my meeting with strangers now wholly familiar to me . . . the medusaean Mrs. Wintermann, the poor feebleminded boy Danny Coyle, and the late Dr. Walther Reindorf, blue-lipped, yellow-faced, outstretched rigid in his casket without a lid.

What ill wind had brought me here? For those of you who know something of my nightmarish story, you may be sure it was a question I would repeatedly ask myself for the next five long years of solitude.

$\sim$

'You've certainly seen better days,' Clorinda miaowed, observing me in the double-breasted princess coat I'd bought two seasons earlier from Bergdorf's.

Untrue! What she actually said was: 'That scarf's seen better days.'

Only the thinnest veneer of friendship prevented her from making her meaning more clear. I clenched my gloved hands.

I was selecting my outfit for a job interview in the Village. I'd set my sights on a little press with a nonetheless legendary imprint.

'You're gonna get that job, cutiepie.' Clorinda smiled unconvincingly. Her eyebrows were plucked, which hindered facial expression. 'No kidding, there's no one cuter.'

'Oh, come on!' I protested.

We had known each other no more than a week, boarders in adjacent rooms at the Webster Residence for Women, then found ourselves competing for copy-editing posts in the same orbit – brittle encounters! – so not unnaturally Clorinda's remarks tended to be double-edged.

Despite these indistinct putdowns, in some mysterious way I got the job.

'Welcome to New York,' the previous incumbent grinned. 'It'll be a great city ... ' She paused. ' ... when they finish building it.'

She was a tall, athletic, *magna cum laude* Vassar girl, and a descendant of one of the early colonists. I learned she was leaving to prepare for her coming out at the annual débutante ball.

She nodded as she hung my coat and scarf on the hat-stand.

'I see you need no lessons in style,' she remarked not unkindly. 'In this trade, it's better to be an oddly dressed person with the wrong hemline than a second-rate version of somebody else.'

When she heard of my success, Clorinda – eyes expressionless – lavished praise. She could afford to. On the same day, she'd landed a much superior editing job at one of the largest mail-order book clubs in the English-speaking world.

Her own success radiated from her. All of a sudden she looked tremendously pretty.

Yet for all her surface sophistication, I thought, the mind of Clorinda was as dull as a spelling bee.

All the same, in spite of myself, I was genuinely impressed by how she could make her influence felt and how, on the strength of her new job, she'd promptly secured a perfect townhouse apartment, with a controlled rent, on the Upper East Side.

So, not without unnameable misgivings, I agreed to share.

In a strange city, I thought, better the devil you know.

∼

'The man's a clown!' I complained.

'He may be a hotshot comma-hound,' Clorinda agreed, a little too eager to show sisterly disdain, 'but sometimes he can be a horse's ass!'

The object of our censure was Sherman Seymour Dane, senior fiction editor at the venerable publishing house where Clorinda was now apprenticed as an aspirant 'book doctor' under Sherman's iron rule.

When Sherman had accepted my second novel, Clorinda

had at once seen her chance to press me into interceding for her.

'He's the most influential ideas man on Publishers' Row,' she'd gloated, laying claim to her dream job as if it were her God-given due.

My intercessions had prevailed; Clorinda was hired, but, foolishly, I never foresaw how I would come to dread the editorial knife wielded by Sherman's star-struck second string.

Sherman called the fiction department his Correctional Facility.

'Do we need all these commas?' had been his first stern remark, crossing out slews of commas on a working proof; he'd had a specimen chapter from my manuscript-in-progress set into galleys.

He shook his massive head. 'Sweetheart, it's just not very snappy, is all.'

Sherman's harsh New York accent was delivered through a blue-chinned out-thrust jaw. He'd then cited, with a quizzical eyebrow, recurrences of the passive voice in my writings.

'Her nights were passed in dreams unlooked for.'

He sat slumped – a ruminant – lips pursed to receive his empty pipe. His thick horned-rimmed eyeglasses were as weighty as his magnum-sized marbled fountainpen.

Clorinda had told me that when Sherman edited a writer's new work his features underwent a kind of transfiguration and he would assume that writer's unique author-shaped head.

Now, secluded in our apartment, she attempted to console me with crocodile tears and epic Gin Slings.

'I think this young woman writes marvelously,' she quoted. 'Those were his own words on the first reader report, remember? Said he admired the fine shifts of gear from one sentence to another. So quit bitchin' about the cuts.'

'He knows what he's doing, right?' Still I doubted.

'If he gets outta line,' Clorinda promised, 'I'll cut him off at the knees.'

～

The next evening, when Clorinda returned to the apartment, she swore she had seen Janis Joplin and Jimi Hendrix that afternoon, 'kinda tangled', leaving the Chelsea Hotel.

'As sure as day I saw them,' she insisted, though I had voiced no disbelief. 'Goofing around as merry as songbirds.'

Remarkably, a week later, I, too, glimpsed the doomed pair strolling by a midtown antiquarian bookstore where I browsed most days on my lunch hour.

A sere yellow leaf had settled on Janis's rebellious hair, and when the wind blew a feathery strand into her eyes they both laughed. She and her spangled troubadour were clinging close, with his long tapered fingers splayed on the shopfront window as they studied a program of lunchtime readings by Lawrence Ferlinghetti.

It was at that moment that I saw an answer to a textual problem that had been troubling me ever since I'd started to draft my new novel's tricky second chapter. The first had been a breeze.

If you are not familiar with the text, *An Auroral Stain* was conceived as a postbellum detective story and built on the fictitious premise of a private investigation by a housebound Emily Dickinson intent to solve the mystery of a serving-woman's suspicious death, ably assisted by Maggie, her faithful Irish maid; my central conceit has the young colleen and her phobic mistress sleuthing as a sort of composite Massachusite Nancy Drew.

Yet, having defined the mechanics of my narrative, I had found myself in a quandary as to how to resolve certain ambivalences in the self-confessed 'dark ideas' that characterized Dickinson's view of black citizens in her post-war Amherst of the late 1860s.

Now, in the bookstore, here under my hand, on the musty page of an early tract, was a vivid documented account unfolding of a Negress flogged with a cat-o'-nine tails for a crime she has not committed.

> The negress was to suffer first. She was dragged from the jail wild with fright and apprehension. The jailer said, 'Forty lashes, sheriff,' the cat was swung slowly up, and the ends of the lashes raked the woman's back, bringing blood at the first blow.

When I glanced again from the page, I was dismayed to find Janis and Jimi had vanished.

For some little time the after-image of Jimi's brilliant grin was all that remained until it, too, faded at last on the vault of the mauve city sky.

∿

'Gimme a break!'

'Simmer down,' I soothed. I'd mildly protested when Clorinda for the third weekend straight had persisted in hanging out with a young girl from a private school upstate she'd met in a bar in the West Village. One time they stayed out all night at a cellar club, one of the seediest caves on Eighth Avenue, because Clorinda knew the maître d'. Somehow they'd returned at dawn from the scene in the boss's limousine.

I was unnerved in the mornings by the girl's appraising kohl-hollowed eyes beneath eyelashes so stiff and immense they seemed like courtship plumage cut out of cardboard. Her slipstream was cigarette smoke and stale Mitsouko.

Half-dressed, hungover and unshowered, the girl had an

effect on me that quickened stirrings of unwelcome passions. Throughout those rancid weekends I'd taken to wearing a black turtleneck top, my rooted neuroses manifest in a chest rash I was alert to cover up whenever I could.

Monday evening, the girl safely immured at school, I turned on Clorinda.

'*You bitch,*' I said in a low, even voice. '*You want me to say, "I quit." But I won't.*'

(*Sudden friendship, sure repentance.* I shivered as I experienced the truth of that wise caution.)

Clorinda was wearing her most foolish smile. She was freshening her makeup at the vanity unit, her face harsh in its unforgiving light. Her clipped, glossy hair had the sheen of a wet squirrel.

'I was wondering what had gotten into you.' She shrugged. 'Now I know.'

It was her invariable ruse to speak in an offhand manner whenever she was unusually intense about anything. That's how she put her critics off their guard.

Since the summer, she'd taken to floating through the apartment in a peach babydoll negligee and, like Marilyn Monroe, she affected to keep her underwear in the refrigerator.

This crass provocativeness, however, had not succeeded in overcoming my unspoken reluctance to share the conquests she brought back from the out-of-the-way bars she nightly prowled downtown.

She, in her turn, would not admit her chagrin at my rejection. Those gray eyes were barricades against emotions.

'First off, you're so impossibly square! A total cube!' Clorinda swept my black felt beret off a coat-peg as she reached for her jacket. 'Stupidest damn thing I ever saw.'

She gave me her little smiling stare, a mask to hint at sweet contrition.

'Aw, dammit, now the day's shot to hell! You wanna start over?' She raised a notional interrogative eyebrow. 'I thought not.'

'Total bullshit! Gedouttahere!' I screamed, all restraint gone.

She stood at the open door, still smiling, at her snidest.

'There too much happenin', kiddo, so why sleep when we might miss a party?' There was a vile note to her voice. She opened her umbrella. 'Gotta run.'

The outer door slammed. I found myself weeping.

I suddenly understood what it was I resented most. It was never being *alone*. A separate room, that's what I was missing, a room in which I could have cried myself to sleep!

I opened my notepad and wrote:

> Clorinda,
> This is a real weird situation. To have one's life, never mind one's clothes, edited by one's antitype is the absurdest fate.
> That's why I'll be gone before you return.
> I tell you, it will be a perfect disappearing act, first chance I get!
> Theresa
> P.S. By the way, next time you want to go through some one else's garbage you'll find my Left Bank beret in the trash.

≈

EVERY CONVENIENCY.

And so it was that early next morning I strode across the Queensboro Bridge, unburdened of all but the clothes I stood up in and a small leather valise in which I'd bundled my latest draft of Chapter Two and a hurriedly packed toiletries bag.

It was the kind of morning, I thought, when one could just do anything and it wouldn't count.

Already this breezeless day and New York's crystalline sky had assumed the sort of hardness and brilliancy of glare that can sometimes flip a cityscape into super-reality.

I blinked to collect my scattered thoughts, and called to mind my aim.

Wanted. A room for rent. I'd ask at every street corner in Queens, if I had to.

And ask I did but to no avail until I reached a newsstand some three miles from the bridge and learned in short order that I was in Irishtown.

'We'll be havin' no corruption of God-fearing people wid sellin' that bleetherin' commie rag!' raged the purple-faced newsvendor, chomping on his cigar. I'd asked for *The New York Times*.

When I told him my true purpose his hostility somewhat abated.

'Ye say ye want a room for the night but take my warnin', ma'am, and go look for it someplace else, or maybe ye'll never see daylight again.'

As I turned away, a mailman called out cheerily enough, 'A room ye want? Best see the parish deacon, so you should.' He indicated a church at the end of an avenue.

Indeed, now I paused to survey the intersection I could see that their God-fearing Irishtown seemed to boast a church on every street corner.

But I was never to reach the sanctuary of a church.

A hundred paces down the avenue a wave of nausea suddenly came upon me and I sought the shade of a canopied entrance.

The sick dizziness would have claimed me then had not someone taken my arm and led me to a chair.

Through a mist I glimpsed the half-formed words of a

sign . . . *& SON FUNERAL HOME INC.*, thereupon I must have fainted.

∾

I sat there, a distraught mourner.

To accept the assumption of this rôle was so much easier, I decided, than the painful embarrassment of owning up.

So to cover my confusion I approached a memorial table arrayed with a silver-plated paper-tissue dispenser and the deceased's personal effects:

> Item: A black-edged card inscribed, *Dr. Walther T. Reindorf. Visitation Tuesday, November 12, from 3:00–8:00pm at Funeral Home (hereunder)*; Item: autographed studio portrait photo of deceased; Item: an open box of Sumatran cigarillos; Item: a dandyish Brooks Brothers amoeba-patterned silk bow tie; Item: a walking cane with a golf-putter-shaped silver cheroot case in the handle . . .

My eye was caught by a medical prescription pad with pink carbon copy flimsies, overstamped with a date a week earlier. The terse message, scrawled in a radiographer's grease pencil, piqued my curiosity:

Walther T. Reindorf, M.D.

Patient: *WALTHER REINDORF*
(PLEASE PRINT)

CIGARILLOS
quant. suff.

Refill *5* times *DAILY AS NEEDED*

DR *WTR*   NOV 5 1968
(DISPENSE AS WRITTEN)

'The old doc's last scrip,' the funeral director observed with a guarded laugh. 'His night-nurse was a man-hating nag.'

He indicated a boy about twelve years old loitering under the canopy. The lad's mouth was agape. There was drool on his chin. His nose needed wiping. The eyes were wide, staring, dull.

''Cept my boy snuck past her regular with a pack of cigars from the mart. Called little Danny his cigar store Indian 'cause, snow or rain, most every day he was running errands for the doc.'

He unfolded a handkerchief.

'Himself,' he added tenderly, 'we call Mister Junior,' then he withdrew to attend to his son.

The boy was simple, *fatuitas infantilis*, I thought, looking at him with keener eyes.

'A soft place in his head he has,' a voice at my shoulder grated. 'The boy is gifted to be different.'

A tall woman, gaunt with age, had sidled up to me. She wore a bulging eyepatch. It reminded me of a phylactery.

Her hair was lank and drawn back severely from her forehead. Her rusty black mourning costume of heavy brocade had narrow pleats in panels down the front and back like scaly reptilian folds.

She took my elbow in a fierce grip and propelled me to the open coffin.

'*So.*' She indicated the corpse's graveclothes. 'The last shirt has no pockets.'

In a strange city, I thought, expect strange things.

'I am, inside my heart, so weary as it is possible.' Her voice was singularly harsh, with speech patterns unfamiliar to me.

'*Mein guter Kamerad* the doctor was,' I heard her confide to the boy as I followed her out on to the sidewalk.

'Doctor, good.' Little Danny repeated slowly her words, as if his mind could reproduce only a slavish echo, being incapable of original thought.

I blinked in the afternoon sunlight and involuntarily blurted out:

'I have been looking for furnished rooms all over the place, yet there is none to be found quite ...'

'... like *ours*,' she completed. *'Natürlich.'*

She pressed a silver half-dollar into the boy's hand then withdrew a bunch of keys from her handbag and, in thirty paces, we reached the steps of her apartment house, a solid 1920s building ornamented with a geometrical frieze of terra cotta and dark brick.

As she fumbled with the lock, the mailman appeared with a handful of letters. He shifted his wad of gum, scratched his head a moment, then muttered:

'Honest truth now. Never seen no roomers here in all of twenty years.'

He placed the mail on the doorstep and I read the name of the addressee:

Mrs. Anneliese Hildegard Wintermann. Realtor.

∾

'Tell me. I should like much to hear,' she said.

'A room to the end of Fall,' I smiled nervously, 'I wish my intentions to be absolutely clear.'

'Absolut klar. We have no other way to be.' The eyes of Mrs. Wintermann had become sharp, piercing, hawk-like. 'And such a room! We have timed this day most luckily!'

In the lobby, she paused outside her ground floor apartment only to unhook a large mortise key from the board above the empty concierge desk.

Numbered keys hung witness to her empty apartments, and yellowing unclaimed letters were stacked in abandoned pigeonholes.

'*Rooms,*' she whispered. '*What for are they and what shall I do with them?*' So close to my ear was her mouth that her voice sounded within my head like an uttered thought of my own.

There was a thickness of dust on every surface; the glimpse I snatched of her living quarters showed a dark parlor as enticing as a musty grotto.

'The laundry there is, then will we go down.' Mrs. Wintermann indicated two cotton drawstring bags. 'Thanks, very.'

We each took a bag and I followed her as quickly as I could into the claustral gloom of a passage flanked by tall, bare clothes-stands.

'It is so kind of you ... ' I began with quickened breath.

'It is to myself I am kind,' she said mysteriously.

The laundry bag soon grew burdensome. The neglect of this old-world walk-up block, it was borne in on me, could also be sensed beneath the pungent odor from the garbage chute, and betrayed by the evident breakdown of the dumbwaiter for the laundry.

The house was peculiarly still.

We descended the stairs to an airless chamber that was as cobwebbed as the bottom of a dry old well.

'Please go where you will,' Mrs. Wintermann said, unlocking an immense bulkhead door. 'Make it as you please. There's every conveniency.'

She turned her face toward me and nodded, a sly smile on her lips. The movement loosed disheveled, matted tresses.

'*Phänomenal!*' she exclaimed with a fractured laugh. 'We are so like, we must be the same.'

Then her voice trembled with a different tenor like a train going over a bridge.

'But these things we know, of course. So Gott will, we shall give much time to our work.'

She switched on a light and motioned me through the bulk-head.

'Thank you, mine better angel,' I heard the madwoman murmur.

They were her last words before the heavy steel door clanged shut behind me and, with sickening dread, I beheld a laundry room that wasn't there.

A key turned in the lock. I was alone. I had found my separate room.

∽

Somehow in her curious delirium Mrs. Wintermann had pulled a classic switcheroo.

I had been expecting bachelorette studio quarters yet found a catacomb of dim chambers defying me to enter, a series of curtained-off lairs each more sinister than the last as I progressed through them.

Before very long I apprehended that I was confined in a subterranean blast shelter built for survival in the event of a nuclear war.

A long incarceration was evidently foreseen.

In one recess stood half a dozen fifty-five-gallon drums of chlorinated water and any number of cartons labeled *Food Rations*, containing dehydrated food bars and sachets of freeze-dried noodles or chowder, all with a twenty-five years' shelf-life.

Stunned, I leafed through a pamphlet tacked to a bulletin board: *The Facts of Fallout*, published by the Federal Civil Defense Administration.

But shaken though I was by these discoveries, it was the contents of the final chamber that chilled my heart.

I looked upon the entrance to the compartment with a mounting unease that forced me wonder afresh at my original fears.

The little alcove room was furnished in the manner of the austerest box-bedroom, crammed with a trundle bed wedged under a writing desk on which perched a *Rheinmetall* portable typewriter.

Above the desk, a framed portrait photo of Erich Honecker scowled down at me. The caption read:

Die Zukunft gehört dem Sozialismus

'The future belongs to socialism,' I breathed.

That East Germany's reviled leader, the execrated ideologue of the Cold War, should be venerated here, in the godliest of the five boroughs, I found truly astonishing.

But a mischievous hand had defaced the image with a radiographer's grease pencil.

One word:

Verführer!

Verführer! Mis-leader! It was an act of subversion that seemed to suggest a confusion of divided loyalties for the room's sometime occupant . . . soon to be confirmed (doubtless you will have guessed) as Dr. Walther T. Reindorf!

The evidence was not far to seek: a drawer of prescription pads printed with his name; countless packs of Sumatran cigarillos; pre-revolutionary Havana cigars in cedar boxes; and a filing cabinet of A-to-Z patient records, whose last stash yielded a confidential report itemizing his 'diagnostic impressions' of Mrs. Anneliese Hildegard Wintermann, madwoman.

Under the heading, 'general oversight', Dr. Reindorf had written:

> The likelihood of a relapse is very high should she discontinue this treatment. I have concluded that the severe manic episodes of this special case can be effectively treated, and contained, only by continuance of the optimum dose administered under my personal supervision.

The answer dawned! Clearly after the doctor's death Mrs. Wintermann had renounced her medication!

Suddenly my throat was so dry I felt I was choking. I found a glass and sipped my first draught of bleached water.

A close reading of the doctor's notes revealed the gravity of Mrs. Wintermann's condition and the depths of my own folly.

Hideous psychopathological terms, as in letters of flame, flickered on the page ... *reduplicative paramnesia, delusional subjective misidentification, intermetamorphosis delusions, psychotic pluralization* ... concluding with the memo, 'Increase Haloperidol, 20 mg *quaque die.*'

In a word, the diagnosis was dire. According to Dr. Reindorf, Mrs. Wintermann in her profound delusion believed that perfect imitations of herself had been sent abroad somehow to share her existence and like Catherine, Empress of Russia, she was quite prepared to see her phantom double walking up and down her throne room and tolerate the imposture.

In the doctor's view of this bizarre symptomatology, his patient believed there were women physically identical with her, in every respect, whose purpose was to protect her from enduring those portions of American urban life that had simply become too unbearable.

'*Yes,*' I shuddered, '*of course! The prospect of surviving a nuclear war alone in this bunker would be enough for any madwoman to conceive a replica of herself as better able to withstand it!*'

I tried to recall Mrs. Wintermann's recent words. 'It is to myself I am kind,' she had said. 'We are so like, we must be the same.'

The conclusions were clear enough.

She had mistaken *me* for her doppelgänger.

~

I wasted no time in examining my dismal prison with an eye to the means of escape.

I fixed in my mind all I saw in the bunker in those first hours of the longest day I ever lived.

The locked bulkhead door was of armor steel plate, reinforced by steel bars, and hung on massive hinges. Embedded in the structure was a chunk of some sort of ballistic-resistant glass. The door was penetrable only by this tiny peep-hole.

As though viewed from the wrong end of a telescope, a diminutive Mrs. Wintermann stared out from the gloom with a grin like a dead hare.

Her eye was fixed on the door as if she would pierce through it.

I never saw a human figure from whom I felt so much inclined to draw back.

As I soon learned, no cries or hammerings can be heard through a fortress-thick shield designed to supposedly withstand a one-megaton nuclear blast in a war of mutually assured destruction.

Yet I saw Mrs. Wintermann's lips move.

'I vill not be so looked at!' I seemed to hear her say, then she briskly removed herself from view.

I sank to my knees in despair. My ears were ringing as if I were deep beneath the sea.

~

RETRIBUTIVE HALLUCINATIONS.
Solitude in a condemned cell subdues the appetite.

A little booklet published by the Federal Civil Defense Administration told me that if I drank three pints of water a day I had a fighting chance of survival.

Nevertheless, sometimes I would forget to eat and drink in a fever of inspired composition, typing like an express train and burning out all the stops in between.

In those early months of my captivity, I wrote most of the core passages of *An Auroral Stain*.

Was it the muffled chiming of the bells from those Irishtown churches on each street corner or the sheer drudgery of my austere day-to-day routines that I found conducive to the mapping of the febrile psyche of the Belle of Amherst and the quaint notions of her resourceful Irish maid?

Sometimes I would hear the faint strains of a fiddle diddlydeeing and it was as if the once hidden roots of a deep-set tree were exposed raw above ground.

Anyhow, the brogue of those Irishtown denizens must have been still ringing in my ears when I wrote:

'A sneeze as long as Nebuchadnezzar!' Maggie scolded as she took her mistress's wet cape and hat.
The maid had been kneeling on the homestead veranda, whitewashing a garden bench in a curious atavistic ritual, as if to welcome a long-lost relation to a hooley.

She took Emily by the elbow and led her, half-fainting, to her room.

That night she attended her mistress in her delirium, hearing her call out strange imprecations: 'Refuse the mediciners, damn you! Why are our people backslidden!'

So wild and convulsed was her expression she was raving a jeremiad.

'There is no medicine against death!' she gasped. 'Take heed, girl, of the promise of a man, for it will run like a crab!'

'By the cross,' Maggie exclaimed, 'there is fey blood i' ye're head! The poor darlin's brain's on fire and full of proclamations!'

In my notes to my novel I encoded 'Emily' as 'Em Dash', both on account of her mercurial nature *and* of her all-pervasive typographical separatrices that signal the places where you should catch your breath before resuming her spare end-stopped verses.

Four months into my immurement I had completed my manuscript of a little over five hundred pages, written at a rate of four pages *quaque die*.

My fingers were raw. The air of that vault so stank with the fug of its unwashed inmate and the shredded litter of moldering snack wrappers that a sow would not have found her own young in the late doctor's trashed den.

～

Since any attempted account of my enforced confinement (which, as you're aware, came to be popularly known as the *Nuke-shelter Spy Nest* affair) has been wholly traduced by the gutter press, I have only now consented to refute their manifest falsehoods with these memories, an impulse sparked I must confess in response to earnest petitioning by one of the few acquaintances of my first days in New York I wholly trust, namely Sofie Devries (*'Hi! Sofie!'*), the urbane Vassarian intern and eager young débutante whose friendly counsel I cherished all those years ago.

So, as promised, these words will be read *first* in Sofie's Phi Beta Kappa alumnae club's quarterly, Fall issue, a scoop denied the sensationalists of the East Coast's yellow press.

∿

How can I describe the silent heartache of those lost lonely years?

Any attempt to escape was about as useless (I can hear Emily the poetess declare) as taking a sword to divide the waters of the Nile.

My only companion was Dr. Reindorf's somber monolithic radio, looming in the corner of his hideaway, a vast Bakelite cabinet manufactured in Stassfurt, East Germany, with tubes that glowed hot through the worn mesh of the speaker grille.

I could depress a row of plastic keys to change the bands but, whatever the frequency, and regardless of my nicety of touch, when I spun the tuning knob the waveband pointer would stick obstinately at the same spot on the dial.

This slippage of the dial cord on its spindle meant I had no choice but to listen to *WRVR* from New York on FM and *Radio Moscow* on shortwave, the broadcasts restricted to those stations where the pointer jammed.

Irreducibly strange, Mrs. Wintermann herself must have been hooked up in her witch's nook upstairs to an auxiliary speaker from the doctor's radio, because promptly at midday she would turn the power on and at five minutes past noon she'd switch the set off.

Thus, for a scant five frustrating minutes each day, I might hear a few snatches of crackling speech telling of the civil rights movement, clashes with segregationists, say, recounted by Adam Clayton Powell, or news of the Kent State outrage, or the Fifth Avenue women's march, or I might hear on the Radio Moscow frequency a string of Russian names repeated with metronomic regularity, '*Mikhail, Evgeniya, Grigory, Dmitry, Boris, Ludmila, Valentin, Sergei, Svetlana,*' etc. in a sequence no less nonsensical than the scat singing on Ed Beach's *Just Jazz* radio show beaming out from Harlem.

On the doctor's desk sat a *Funk & Wagnalls Practical Standard Dictionary*, over three inches thick, the pages notched with a thumb-tabbed index, like little footholds cut into a mountainside.

Curiously, someone had added a double-indexing system with snippets of colored wooden spills glued to seemingly random pages, yet grubby and worn from habitual use.

I suspected the volume held the key to decryption of secret messages, which no doubt emanated ultimately from Soviet spymasters in the Deutsche Demokratische Republik, and for many hours I tried unavailingly to fathom the principle underlying these mysterious transmissions.

Yet what would have been the point of decipherment when you honestly feel you are as worthless as a person in a botched federal witness protection program whose minders have thrown away the key?

The Germans have an apt saying for such furtive concealment.

Eine Leiche im Keller haben. To have a corpse in the basement.

≈

To say my *only* companion in that dismal oubliette was Dr. Reindorf's Stassfurt radio is to mis-speak.

A black rubber bezel, sealed to the wall of the entry-chamber, enclosed an eyepiece labeled *Periskop*.

I very soon learned the reason for the defunct laundry shaft: Its conversion to a periscopic conduit to the roof of Mrs. Wintermann's boarding house not only granted me sight of the street but also permitted the radio antenna-wire to run through the same aperture.

Who, then, was my more constant companion of those stolen years?

As loyal as the terrier that pined for more than a decade at his master's grave, little Danny Coyle stood sentinel all day, and every day, at his post outside his father's funeral home.

The fixed lens disclosed a quadrant of bright grass, a glimpse of the canvas entry canopy, and the church walk that led to a chancel door.

'Doctor, good,' little Danny had once repeated in my hearing. Did the boy, like the dog, mourn his master, I wondered, waiting for the return of Dr. Reindorf, to hear again a kind word or bluff command to obey?

Outside, the leaves of the trees were still, still as the bricks sleeping in the walls of my prison.

I thought: *'No different from Danny, I am sentenced to stare all day at a dumb brick wall.'*

~

'He's a grand little fella but not the full shilling.'

In my reverie in the funeral home's reposing room I had listened without thought to the hushed chatter of the mourners. I understood now, in the perfect seclusion of my meditative state, that they had been speaking of young Danny.

'A divarsion like, for the doc, so the lad was.'

'To run a message for his smokes? Was the doc not drunk as a fiddler's bitch intirely?'

'Now that wouldn't be seriously you're talking? Sure the doc was a darlin' fine man!'

'Aye right, a good skin and gone in a mortal instant.'

The boy's attire was unchanging, regardless of season: a herringbone newsboy cap, back-to-front, and moss-green windbreaker, which was designed almost by intent, I began to think, to dissolve into the background of the ivy-clad walls that defined the fringe of the church next door.

One Monday in late February I observed three women pass the church's side entry and pause to address Danny. They were wearing those little black lace mantillas, required of devotional women in those days, and bearing armfuls of yellowing, dried palm leaves.

You may be familiar with my little fable, *Ash Monday*? (An eminent critic, I may say, described it as 'instinct with a delicacy of feeling to rival *Dubliners*.')

In that tale the guileless young boy with blank eyes is named Conal, and I wrote his tragic history in a frenetic all-nighter, dressed in Dr. Reindorf's lavender tie and mustard yellow waistcoat, and fueled by a double ration of a dehydrated multi-purpose meal extracted from soybean, which I now learn was formulated by nutritionists to feed lepers.

I had watched from my secret conning tower as little Danny, his dead palm leaves held reverently in a sheaf, passed from my sight, bound for the chancel door.

> Sister Immaculata was waiting in the furnace room under the presbytery.
>
> A stove had been lit in one corner of the basement.
>
> In the seven years Conal had known the nun she had never once thanked him for a task performed aright.

Her more articulate pupils at the parish school had learned very soon she never, but never, expressed gratitude, strong in her belief that such license falsely gave countenance to the sin of self-exaltation.

Despite her stern regard, her mouth softened, head inclined at a resigned angle.

'Don't think bad o' my saying the truth to the likes o' you,' she muttered, 'but sure it's no great thing and raison to be proud that ye do ye're best.'

She gestured to an open wicker laundry basket where bunches of withered palm leaves were stowed in readiness for the flames.

A pair of heavy kitchen scissors were to hand for clipping the fronds.

Conal hesitated. Until that morning his palm leaves had been pressed under the mattress of his parents' marital bed, and the boy had been told they were sacred artefacts possessing miraculous healing powers no less divine than those of a holy reliquary.

'Indade, ye're a dacint spalpeen, Mister Junior, and sure we'd be lost widout ye. Thank ye kindly and God's blessing be wid ye.'

Abruptly, Sister Immaculata snatched the magic palms from Conal's grasp and tossed them into the maw of the potbelly stove. Consigned to the blaze, his votive gift at once shriveled into Wednesday's ashes.

There was a shuddering gasp.

Conal seized the scissors, lurched toward her, clumsily, menacingly, and lunged ...

Well, it's possible you know the rest, Sofie ... my sketch here is just to show you how swiftly a prisoner is reconciled to retributive hallucinations!

∾

With the passing of time, month succeeding month, I

became accustomed to my cage, my hatred of my betrayer slowly blunted, and so a new desire to live asserted itself.

For each dragging minute there was one true constancy, attendant every daylight hour, who stood like a lump of clay at his post, a few yards from my prison, out of hearing but within my sight to tantalize my senses . . . yes, Dr. Reindorf's cigar store Indian, munching White Castle hamburgers.

'Himself' standing there was a comfort. Staunch little Danny Coyle.

Then one day in March, some four months after my entrapment, I was astonished to see through my spyglass a figure – recognizable by his tan homburg hat – approach the boy . . . *Sherman Seymour Dane!*

In my closed, silent world, where the squeakings of a cupboard door were the consolations of an intimate friend, I clamored for communion with even that most formidable of mentors; I was near to sinking into a faint from a rush of blood to the head.

I recovered to see Sherman hold out a photo for the boy to inspect; Danny stared dully, making no response but to blink and remain very still.

I heard no words yet they sounded in my mind.

$\sim$

Act 1, Scene 1: Irishtown. A street intersection. *Time:* midmorning. A church clock chimes the hour. A *man* and *boy* occupy center stage with uneasy exchanges.

Sherman: 'Find this lady and we're talking big bucks.'

He taps the photo. The Adam's apple of the *boy* is seen to bob as he gulps.

From the corner delicatessen *Mrs. Wintermann* emerges. We can spy an enticing sauerkraut barrel within. *Sherman* (resuming his house-to-house inquiries) approaches this fresh interlocutor to repeat his questioning.

The *boy* appeals to *Mrs. W.*, his head thrown back in the sunlight so the pronounced thyroid cartilage beneath his chin projects like a second nose.

Danny: 'The man was funning me.'

Mrs. Wintermann: 'I never did ever see suchlike a woman before.'

~

Well, Sofie, that's what I imagined my captor said, and years' later Sherman's own account of his blighted attempt to trace me did not materially differ from my own.

In a trance, I watched Mrs. Wintermann shake her head and walk away.

It seemed just by stretching forth a hand I could tweak Sherman by the nose without any effort.

(Afterward, I learned how, when he received my second chapter of *An Auroral Stain*, he had studied the postmark on the package I'd mailed that first day in Irishtown and concluded I was somewhere in the easternmost neighborhood of the 108th Precinct.)

But on that March morning of my deepest despair, I knew only that Sherman's crestfallen demeanor signaled his defeat as he seated himself on a street bench, adjusted the strides of his leather pants, and flourished a white handkerchief to polish his Coke-bottle eyeglasses.

I had misjudged him, I remember I chided myself. Totally.

Rival publishers had gibed at the man, dubbing him *The Shaman*, for his magical knack of conjuring up bestsellers; privately, I had called him the Great Sham.

Now, to my shame, I was rapidly revising my assumptions.

His fastidiousness I now understood to be conscientiousness, and I viewed him through a distinctly softer focus when he picked up his hat and brushed the underside of the crown in that finicky way he has, preparatory to taking his leave.

Sherman favored at that time an absurd ensemble of a fringed leather jacket with matching fringed leather trousers girded with a garrison belt. In beaded buckskin he looked less masculine than Calamity Jane. On Sherman's birthday, one of the English authors in our publishing stable had sent him a card pointedly inscribed, *'To the best of chaps!'*

'Yes,' I murmured with a whimper, as Sherman departed the stage before the scene changed to Desolation Row, *'Dear Sherman. The best of chaps!'*

~

After that catastrophic reverse, I became possessed of the fear that the translucent membrane that separates the inner world and outer world was dissolving.

Blood hummed in my ears as through my bulkhead spyhole I would see an indistinct figure detach itself from the gloom of the antechamber to fix a baleful eye on my prison door.

The sight of Mrs. Wintermann was the more ghastly for the appearance of a rodent ulcer that shone beneath her eyepatch like the inside of a mussel shell.

'She is a woman,' I thought, *'who carried live coals in her breast.'*

Strange thoughts were knocking at the door of my mind, and at night I dreamt my cell was visited by dark-hooded angels who hovered over my bed.

In the faces of those Angels of Angst were fused the features of Janis Joplin, Emily Dickinson, and Sylvia Plath, a composite mask that expressed a certain pasty sleeplessness due, no doubt, to their midnight lucubrations.

I began to see them as malevolent birds of prey.

'They cover me with their wings,' I thought, *'and tear me with varnished talons.'*

Their psychical resemblance and hormonal reality I could not account for, lest it were their concerted will toward self-murder. I wrestled these angels with ridicule. To my mind, the ludicrousness of Dickinson's Empress of Calvary was exceeded only by the pallid self-pity of Plath's Lady Lazarus.

(Anyhow, I preferred the verses of Karen Gershon, a poetess who in my own view eclipsed Plath in gravitas, insofar as Gershon was in actuality a Jewess and had no need for maudlin notionality.)

My three midnight angels had bright brown eyes like polished leather.

My own weeping red-rimmed eyes were as alluring as smallpox pustules.

My face, like theirs, was pale. Fearfully pale.

~

For months I prayed to His Divine Nothingness.

I learned to hold my breath, mid-breath between divine inhalation and mortal expiration.

Thus much may be sufficient to convey the hideous sense of being watched, the strange and awful hypnotism, almost, of prison walls that robbed me of all initiative.

And, *always*, the dreadful sense that my natural impulses had been reduced to my crouching in a dark corner, a half-drowned bird with limp wings.

~

A GIMLET HOLE.

Then it was spring again, and the swallows arrived within

hailing distance of my burrow, building their nests under the church eaves, just beneath the level of Dr. Reindorf's spyglass in the roof.

It was the fifteenth day of April (the very day, I was reminded, that Belsen concentration camp was liberated, and barely twenty-five years after Anne Frank perished there).

How effortlessly the swallows dipped and skimmed over the funeral home's canopy.

A clod of cold mud had fallen from the raised beds of shrubs that edged the church walk. In five days the swallows had their nests of mud pellets readied for lining.

Like little Danny, I found the fledglings irresistibly cute when they thrust their heads out of their tiny mud caverns.

My field of vision in my *camera obscura* was a silent movie without subtitles. Except, far off, I'd sometimes hear the sharp whistle of the Long Island Railroad trains trundling over the Irishtown El.

At other times I'd hear the faint ringing of day-shift bells from the Bulova watch workshops.

At 8 am. At 12 noon. And at 4:45 pm, when the workday ended. Soon I'd see the men returning to the street, swinging their lunch pails.

'America runs on Bulova Time.'

How true, too, for the condemned of Irishtown!

'At the tone, it's Bulova watch time.'

And watch time I did, communing with the bleakest distance.

When hope takes a vacation the soul seeps out in a sluggish expenditure of wasted time.

There could be no comfort for little moss-green Danny and myself, sentenced together to the same punishment.

'And so, as kinsmen met a night, we talked between the rooms, until the moss had reached our lips, and covered up our names.

~

'Jesus H. Christ!'

Then a weary laconic voice from the Bronx answered, '*He ain't gonna help us none, pal.*'

If you remember, Sofie, those words appeared last year in my op-ed meditation on New York's suburban kitsch, affectionately titled *Musée des Boze Artz,* in which I sketched a day out with Clorinda to Flushing Meadows, trapped, stunned by a heatwave, in a grossly overcrowded subway train.

Clorinda was offered a seat, of course. Jump on a train or enter a bar with Clorinda and guys would at once start coming on to her; but never on to me.

Boze Artz, lest we forget, was a TV store surmounted by a vast sign on the corner of 48th Street and Queens Boulevard at the point where the subway train rounds the curve.

My *Boze Artz* feature was my first published think piece after my discharge from rehab, the reading of which, Sofie, as you'll recall, spurred you to entreat an authentic account of events the *Post* made a front-page screamer:

BURIED ALIVE!
RECLUSE SAVED
FROM SECRET
NUKE BUNKER!

How did I engineer my escape? Have patience, Sofie! See how few pages remain before your curiosity is satisfied! I am sure you will hear me out.

~

They say that treachery in the end betrays itself.

The truth of this adage you may judge yourself when you consider the fortunes and misfortunes of Clorinda, the alley cat.

'*He* ain't gonna help us none, pal!'

Three schoolgirls, crushed together with Clorinda in the subway car, had joined in the sudden outburst of nervous laughter on that day we went to Shea to see the Mets. The heat inside the car was in the high eighties.

Clorinda was quick to strike a rapport with the boldest girl and soon their talk turned to teenage daydreams of early marriage.

A billboard whizzed by: oddly attenuated cigarettes for the liberated young woman.

Virginia Slims. You've come a long way, baby.

The hippest schoolgirl shook her head.

'Whoa! Slow down! So wadda ya s'posed to do when ya tire of Mr. Right?'

'Well,' said Clorinda, with her calculating smile. 'There are always grounds for alimony.'

'Yeah.' The girl's eyes widened. 'Reno. Sounds like a plan.'

(As Sherman once confided to me: 'Life's all about numbers with Clorinda.')

Yes, Clorinda was, indeed, a brazen article of shameless assurance, and it was with this former roommate of mine, who was never seen to lack audacity, that my salvation was irrevocably bound up.

∾

How misguided was Emily in her belief that one could sing '*to keep the dark away.*'

No. *Hate* keeps the dark away: the fierce hate of a wild creature caged, a lone animal pitting its instincts against an all-powerful custodian.

An orange light burned in the antechamber, and I sneaked a peek at Mrs. Wintermann, lurking in her best array at her customary station near the foot of the stairs.

It was one of those bitter New York days of winter; the temperature outside registered on the gauge as near zero, at least according to the dial of Dr. Reindorf's rudimentary *Fahrenheit-Skala*.

Icicles hung from the crumbling plaster ceiling. The walls of my cell were battleship gray. My inhalations drove sharp stabs into my breast-bone.

I was consumed by the fear that Dr. Reindorf's patient would remain forever undiagnosed.

Analyze Anneliese the Ice-Hearted Winterwoman? Impossible!

I gazed down at my jutting ribcage, wasted arms and shrunken thighs. Even when well-fed, my body is of Düreresque proportions; I have a narrow chest; it's as though the Celestial Glassblower failed to catch His breath and abandoned my rightful hourglass figure when it was only half-formed.

My whole frame shuddered in paroxysms of acrimony, blinding my reason.

Through Dr. Reindorf's *Periskop* I could see chain link fences, blue workshirts frozen on washing lines, and yard dogs going on with their doggy lives behind houses of aluminum cladding. It was the fifth year of my captivity.

Shivering, blowing on hands that trembled, I returned to Dr. Reindorf's faithful old *Rheinmetall* typewriter and my dull pain.

Wound on the cylinder was my daily five-finger-*feuilleton*:

a reminiscence of the travails of apartment-hunting in Manhattan with Clorinda; our failed sealed-bid offers of key-money.

(Sometimes she was as charmless as a brick but, on this occasion, she'd charmed a compositor at *The New York Times* and we'd gone to the composing room one Friday afternoon, at the hour the Sunday real estate ads were assembled, and outflanked the perfumed theater crowds on Broadway who'd vie with the weeklies' paragraphists to read the first edition when it hit the streets around 9 pm. We'd heard the presses rumble into life deep underground then felt the building tremble beneath our feet.)

The typewriter had a German Qwertz keyboard so my touch-typing looked like this: *The quick brown fox jumped over the layz dog.*

For umlauted vowels there were separate keys in place of my fraction and colon keys, which additionally marred my text with less than clean results.

Yet, as I typed, I experienced an almost imperceptible pang of hope, like the unaccustomed wag of the tail of a rheumatic dog . . . or of a layz dog, if you will.

A never-before-seen narrow shaft of sunlight cleaved a path through the dust motes, and drove the beam of a new dawn into my throbbing heart. Bright as a gimlet hole bored in the lining of a coffin was the source.

Did this strange radiance announce redemption for the prematurely interred?

Outside, it seems, the ice contracting had opened up a once-sealed overflow spout from a water tank long since removed.

A current of fresh chill air flowed through the new opening and I took my first deep breath of freedom.

A disc of light revealed the faint gray dawn and, at eye level, a quadrant of snow-blanketed grass between the funeral home and the church.

It struck me forcibly that my deliverance was in sight.

I sped to Dr. Reindorf's bolt hole and, my brain on fire, I drafted my first proclamation to the world after one thousand, eight hundred and sixty-one days of silence.

This message I furled tightly round a makeshift projectile I assembled on Dr. Reindorf's desk.

A glance through my periscope confirmed the arrival of faithful young Danny Coyle, wrapped in a hooded parka, at his post for sentry-go.

My face had a ghastly pallor as I inserted the puny missile into my primitive torpedo tube, the newly exposed drainage spout. Channeled through four feet of reinforced wall, the pipe by great good fortune was aimed at Danny's feet.

In one of Dr. Reindorf's closets I'd found a pitcher's glove. On that day at Shea Stadium, Nolan Ryan, the Mets' ferocious high-velocity pitcher, had been the game's star player, and I remembered the heroics of that hard-throwing right-hander who could hurl a baseball at over one hundred miles an hour.

I struck my projectile fiercely on its blunt end and the thing hit its mark with my first shot at twenty paces.

≈

The day they found me was the coldest day ever recorded in Irishtown.

In the street two gum-trees had been leveled by the weight of snow, and power lines were down at the intersection.

What was the truth of the *'Horror-Squalor!'* inside the bunker described by the *Post* so graphically?

Yes. It is true that when the outer door was breached I was drinking Dr. Reindorf's exceedingly rare 1928 vintage

Pol Roger, a champagne he'd almost certainly reserved for when he hit rock bottom in the depths of a nuclear winter.

It's true, too, that there was no covering for my emaciated body but my damp and draggled Bergdorf double-breasted princess coat. On my feet were Dr. Reindorf's elegant hunting boots with their distinctive yellow fold-down cuffs.

I had willed my fragile, imperious bearing not to betray the doubts I'd surely felt in my impulsive ruse when I fired off one of Dr. Reindorf's five cent cigarillos from the disused water spout as from the barrel of a gun.

But I'd hit a home run out of the park and won!

Loyal little Danny had brightened quite wonderfully when he recognized Dr. Reindorf's scrawl in radiographer's grease pencil on the scrip fastened to the cigar band, and off he'd trotted smartly to the tobacco kiosk in the mart.

If I doubted anything, I feared a bird would, crow-like, snatch the paper from the message-bearer.

You may imagine the contents of that medical prescription, Sofie, because that message in a dead hand from the grave, signed and stamped with a date five years after the burial of the signatory, was persuasive enough to bring the cavalry.

$\sim$

'Only thing he's gonna give ya, sister, is a prayer for ya last rites!'

The clerk from the cigar store brushed aside the priest.

Blood clung to my throat like warm silk.

'May the peace of heaven be her sowl's rest, the illigant lady,' the priest persisted.

The restless, twitching lips of Mrs. Wintermann framed a question.

'What for do you with me?' she shrieked.

For a glint of an instant I tried to outface that fierce stare of my mirrored adversary, an instant I do not have the will to forget.

Then her nose drooped like molten tallow and a patrolman led away the jailor who had once thought to seal my fate.

I was comforted by the fact that most of Stalin's doubles (and he had many) outlived their master.

In her wake remained a pungent and highly offensive odor.

～

'Today,' I whispered. 'What a joy after yesterday.'

I shook little Danny's mittened hand. I saw him hatless for the first time and ran my fingers through his carroty hair. I had no silver half-dollar to press into his palm, so I unclipped my only graduation gift, my dainty bracelet watch (a Bulova, aptly enough), and fastened it round his slender wrist.

'You and I,' I murmured, 'like some strange race wrecked, solitary, here.'

Sofie, this is my first attempt at this narrative (or, as the Russians say, a first pancake, piervy blin, which usually is not very good). I can see plainly how I could have told my tale better.

The Press, as you know, has not been kind to me.

Because of my crack-up many have thought I wasn't made for fortitude.

The oft-published photos of my subterranean study, taken soon after my reappearance, reveal a dungeon trampled over by heedless newshounds – a wanton act of destruction that later drew comparisons with the behavior of press cameramen who overran the jungle hideout of that Japanese lieutenant who'd holed himself up for thirty years on an island in the Philippines rather than accept the dishonor of surrender.

In the photos my face is as gray as a rat in a cellar starved of light, my limbs are as white as paper, for my life for so long had been no more than that of a rat burrowing under the floor.

How easy it is for critics to condemn the inertia of my confinement, to impute that standing pools gather filth and that my writings now are as drained of promise as the vitiated atmosphere of my cell.

Let me tell you here that to exact such refinements from a rat sealed in a living grave is as futile as trying to cure its hunger with the twenty-nine cent tube of Unguentine I had thought to pack in my toiletries bag.

No. No one can exorcise the stench of prison that clings to one's mind long after one is free.

My prophetic debut novel, *The Girl Who Got Away*, championed by Sherman, had been a modest *succès d'estime* before my captivity, yet no one then remarked how its theme so closely shadowed my own tragedy of bereavement at the death of my parents who were never to see me reach my teens.

Although death of one's parent is not, legally, abandonment, an orphanage or foster care would have been my prison had not my paternal grandmother taken me in. Her death and my subsequent bamboozling of the child welfare officials to convince them she yet lived should tell you that I am no stranger to masquerading for half a decade in a House of the Dead.

Clorinda had always misjudged my misspent strength and could never have truly gauged my capacity for survival, for the nature of my return was a resurrection for which she could not possibly have been prepared.

As you shall see, for the first time in her shabby life that shallows-dwelling fish was thoroughly unnerved.

~

L'INCONNUE OF THE EAST RIVER.

'For Chrissakes, Shermie, keep your shirt on!'

The thin partitions that separated Sherman from the desk of Clorinda and those of other editors in his Correctional Facility permitted the occupants to be heard but not seen, so my return to our publishing house passed unnoticed.

'You're talking a whole bunch of crazy stuff,' I heard Sherman growl from his cubbyhole of an office.

Clorinda's shingled hair, shiny and crisply cut, shook wildly above the screen.

Try to imagine her horror when she heard I'd risen from the dead!

What a piece of work Clorinda was! You will scarcely believe it, Sofie, but for all those years, sentenced to misery in my solitary cell, I had been duped unawares because most of that time she had been playing a triple game of backstabbing, the little tramp!

To my astonishment, when I'd entered the office, I'd been confronted by hardback and softcover first editions of *An Auroral Stain* by Theresa Ollivante lined up prominently in the display cabinet!

Published! The novel for which Sherman had received only two chapters before my identity had been extinguished by the slamming of my cell door!

The explanation? Five days after my acrimonious departure from our apartment, the drowned naked body of an unknown young female had been found in the river on the Lower East Side.

Clorinda had read the stop-press report and made up her mind to misconstrue the tragedy.

'Y-y-your last note, Theresa!' Clorinda blustered, the

muscles of her face working in the oddest fashion. 'You wrote that your leaving would be a perfect *disappearing act* the first chance you got. What *was* I to think?'

She had visited the morgue to view *L'Inconnue* of the East River.

'There was weed in her teeth. The poor kid's fingers were ribbed from their long soaking in the river. The clincher was the ... ' she hesitated with a twisted smile ' ... the ... uh ... unique peculiarities of her physique.'

She laughed unnaturally, then simpered. Her cheeks burned. Clorinda has tiny child-like nostrils that quiver with disdain, and her laughter revealed exceedingly small even teeth.

'After a month had passed, and no relation of yours had claimed the body of Jane Doe, I thought I owed it to you to pick up your story at the third chapter, along the lines you'd always proposed.' She turned in appeal to Sherman. 'Theresa always wrote note-perfect synopses of every chapter with the whole plot meticulously mapped out.'

So while little Miss Wallflower had ended up in the slammer, choking on a dehydrated ham and egg omelet with a side order of instant white rice, Sherman's Gal Friday had from my notes recomposed my entire novel and hit big with it!

Somewhere, in another office, a radio was softly playing *A Whiter Shade of Pale*. Clorinda was looking kind of seasick.

'This is the parting of the ways,' Sherman pronounced.

Sherman's cavernous voice – usually drawling, amused, and dragging out certain syllables – was now curt, implacable. There was something in the set of his eyes which told her there would be no second chance.

'The serial comma is often a matter of temperament.' My editor grinned at me sheepishly. 'I guess I was led to believe the erratic punctuation that had begun to creep into those typescripts was the product of an eccentric recluse, and just one of the aberrations to which Clorinda claimed you had succumbed!'

Since I was thirteen I have found certain men have looked at me as a woodman will look at the growth of a tree singled out for felling.

Sherman looked at me beneath his shaggy brows as if I were a tree he commended as one that should prosper.

'Didn't you say that being edited sometimes feels like having one's bones reset on a torture rack?' I said in a breaking voice.

'Uh-huh. Sure.'

'I thought I was weaving gold threads from straw and stitching a glorious raiment, but there was Clorinda at my back snipping off all my sequins.'

Sherman plunked down a pile of tear sheets. My reviews.

'What can I tellya?' he grunted, teeth gripping his empty pipe. 'It's been a monumental screw-up. Gonna find an exit strategy, then we'll reschedule.'

He stared again at his favorite Saul Steinberg cartoon behind his desk and grinned.

I smiled, too. I was confident I had no more need to think of Irishtown.

My strange past was over and I was stepping into my stranger present.

$\sim$

AFTERWORD
EDITRIX SOFIE DEVRIES WRITES:

Since receipt of this narrative, promised by Theresa two years' ago (*before* her second nervous collapse and following the issue of her authorized edition of *An Auroral Stain*) she has written once more to draw our attention to the paradox that arises from her attempts to synthesize the estimated two million words she wrote in those years of isolation, a period not dissimilar to the length of incarceration suffered in Sachsenhausen concentration camp during WWII by the son of the Norwegian polar explorer Nansen.

The published diary of Nansen *fils* runs to 600 pages yet his bulky edited volume, recording in detail those years of daily witness to unimaginable horrors, amounts to only *one-third* of the original manuscript.

Like the wartime diarist, Theresa has found the task of distillation is more time consuming than the task of composition. As she says, despairingly, 'It's as though I have all the concordances to the Bible and Shakespeare but not the Works themselves.'

We instance the conclusion of her last letter to us as representative of her predicament:

> I could never go back to Irishtown, Sofie.
>
> To catalog my impressions of even the very first day of that crazed journey into the American psyche would take a year, according to the Law of Relativity defined by Tristram Shandy, who in a 'twelve-month' of writing his autobiography got *'no farther than* [his] *first day's life'* at his birth.
>
> How can I distill the metallic reek of brilliantine, burnished grime, and desperate testosterone that the subway station breathed when I walked under the El? Or the odor of pine-wood, camphor and of ceremonialized death when I recall Dr. Reindorf in his casket?
>
> And could I fully document the ephemera packed by Dr. Reindorf within my prison walls? The instruction manual for his Geiger survey meter? His diet sheets? His shortwave log books.
>
> How, for example, does one attempt to explain the thousands of US dollar bills bundled in wrappers labeled *Deutsche*

Notenbank: Deutsche Demokratische Republik stacked in the Widow Wintermann's bunker-boudoir, next door to Dr. Reindorf's nerve center?

In no government report of the breaching of the bunker is there an itemization of the contents of the Wintermanns' double wardrobe.

So you will not find a detailed description of the late Mr. Wintermann's knife-edge-pressed uniform of steel-blue gabardine, which hung there . . . the uniform of a senior security guard once appointed to the Secretariat Building of the United Nations headquarters in New York City.

There were no collar tabs, yet the cut of his jacket, when contemplated in the dim light of my prison cell, would not have disgraced a Stasi officer of the GDR. A chain hung from his right breast pocket. An emergency whistle! A whistle I blew periodically without effect.

It can be no coincidence, then, that Mrs. Wintermann's chromium breakfast bar in the bunker had as its backdrop a photo-mural of the UN's headquarters, the skyline of the HQ complex viewed from the East River. (*Spywatchers and spycatchers note also:* plastered all over this panorama were scribbled address labels, assigning the names of ambassadors, delegates and members of the secretariat to offices at each level of the administrative skyscraper.)

Yet in no press account of the spy nest have I seen recorded the reasons underlying the choice of Irishtown for the spy ring's 'sleeper agents'.

Irishtown! Even now, I continue to speculate on the cunning of Dr. Reindorf and his East German masters. It is my belief they chose for their spy cell a neighborhood that was already shielded from closer inquiry by a cultural stockade, defiant of the reach of federal intelligence bureaux whose pursuit of home-grown terrorism had led them to look the other way.

How else to explain the handbills for Noraid testimonial nights and fundraising dinners so boldly displayed in the windows of the Irishtown taverns I passed that first afternoon? Often, too, pasted up on washeteria doors, were *In Memorium* notices for revolutionary republicans killed in a guerrilla war three thousand miles away.

Drug-addled Vietnam vets, hunkered down at the curbside to stare into the phantasmagorical depths of puddles, would exchange peace signs with delivery men.

'Peace, brother.'

In the soda fountain, the counter was operated by two survivors of an earlier war. If you looked closely, you could see serial numbers tattooed on their forearms.

So many cultures congregated at that crossroads outside my prison. In the Chinese laundry opposite, the day's receipts were totaled with dizzying speed on an abacus.

Sometimes, I imagined I smelled the swooningly dense rubber gum from the shoe repairman's shop across the street. The thrifty residents of Irishtown could have heel taps fixed to their shoes for five cents while they waited in one of his miniature booths, protected by the modesty screen of a wooden batwing door.

I imagined, too, I smelled the kerosene lights placed by Con Ed at night when digging up the road, or felt the spray on my face from the water trucks sprinkling those streets in high summer.

A decade earlier, before my incarceration, I had not apprehended that the meaningful meaninglessness of a recurrent street corner, which Antonioni dwells on so remorselessly in his movie, *L'Eclisse*, was to recur in my own life as the emotional blotting paper he intended it to be, a bland suburban intersection sopping up each day all dying passions as dusk turns into night . . . the bright unbearable reality, which existentialists call enargeia.

Being buried alive in the blues, Sofie, is a real weird situation.

Filename: **Kepler von Thul**
Classification: **Opiumism**

A BAD CASE
THE UNEXPLAINED GROWING PAINS OF ELISE VON ALPENBERG

'Have you guessed the riddle yet?' the Hatter said, turning to Alice again.

'No, I give it up,' Alice replied: 'what's the answer?'

'I haven't the slightest idea,' said the Hatter.

Alice's Adventures in Wonderland
by Lewis Carroll (1865)

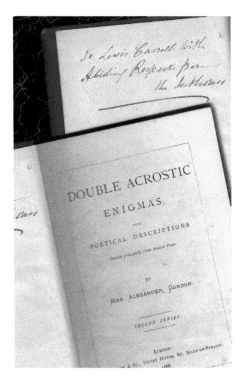

A BAD CASE

THE UNEXPLAINED GROWING
PAINS OF ELISE VON ALPENBERG

You will not find the name of Kepler von Thul in any of
the published, or indeed unpublished, correspondence and
private papers of the Revd. Charles Lutwidge Dodgson (the
baptismal mask that hid the true mask of Lewis Carroll, the
creator of *Alice*), an omission no doubt due to high-minded
censors who have deliberately effaced this German folklor-
ist and eminent mathematician, once known intimately to
Carroll, from all acknowledged Carrolliana presently indexed
by hagiographical scholars.

So I can scarcely find fitting words to tell you that lately
certain documents have come to hand (to *my* hand alone, in
fact) replete with evidence to grant us the privilege of remedy-
ing this puzzling lacuna.

There were three mailed packets addressed to Lewis Carroll
it was my good fortune to purchase in a private sale as a single
lot. All bear the Christ Church address of this celebrated
Oxford mathematics don.

The first, a parcel, half torn open, postmarked 1868, containing a mint unread copy of *Double Acrostic Enigmas* by Mrs.
Alexander Gordon, published in the same year for the benefit
of the Brompton Hospital for Consumption, and signed, *To*

Lewis Carroll with Abiding Respects from the Authoress, holds no interest for me.

The second, a mailed envelope, wax seal broken, franked 1863, containing a manuscript leaf of Leibnitzian logical calculi, concluding with exclamation, *Credo quia absurdum est!* ['I believe it because it is absurd!'] signed, *Kepler von Thul, Oktober 9 1863, Leipzig*; this also need not concern us here.

The third, a letter, wax seal broken, to Lewis Carroll from Kepler von Thul written a week earlier from Leipzig, I reproduce entire below.

∼

Universität Leipzig
Freitag 2 Oktober 1863

My dear Dodo, [The familiar name of Dodgson, a stammerer, whose affliction it immortalised.]

How fondly I recall that feverish day in June, the sudden shower, and our pell-mell dash across the bridge, the three of us squeezed in a hansom, with less than a second to spare to catch the last first class train to London!

And how guilty our smiles when stern scruple detained your clerical chum to pay off our cab fare!

'*Virtus in arduis*, my good fellow!' I sang out gaily to Duckworth from the train, and glad I was to see the good preacher stranded at the railhead, quite vainly attempting to leap aboard, since surely fate had conspired to bestow on him a most cautionary subject for his next sermon? [The Reverend Robinson Duckworth.]

So then all at once there were not three travellers bound for London, but *two*, and in truth I marvelled at how this adventitious operation of subtraction had so perfectly reduced three-ness as to summarily permit our dialectic of *two-ness* to continue delightfully unhindered on our journey.

'Anyhow, all good things come in twos,' I recall remarking. This was the sum of my thoughts as I flung myself into a corner seat, eager to keep the snug carriage to ourselves.

For some time in silence you feebly smoothed the creases of your damp muffler folded on your lap.

You were looking solemn, your pale grey eyes anxiously fixed on your task, as though you felt sure you would catch a bad cold if the thing were not dry very soon.

'Your visit was an unexpected pleasure,' you said at last.

'Kind of you to say so.'

'No unexpected pleasure displeases us,' you responded with a delicate circumspection, which sounded glib considering the offhand dismissal of my academic credentials by your Dean.

(To think my distinguished submissions for a visiting lectureship had foundered simply because of some arcane rule which invalidates any candidate who is not ordained clergy!)

'Your college statutes are positively medieval!'

I could not refrain from another outburst:

'When we rowed past Christ Church Meadow I contend that even your ducks on each side of the river bank spoke Latin.'

'Undi*quaque-quaqua*versus!' you quipped.

However, I have to concede your goodself and the Dean had handed me an altogether greater consolation prize. Our boating expedition upriver with the Dean's three little daughters was rapture unalloyed.

Seated in the train, I watched you remove a notebook from your pocket and resume your jottings.

'Yes, how those ducks repeat their lessons,' you said archly.

'They might as well be at school so much do they like showing off their knowledge.'

Tho' I saw the opening of your notebook was but a ruse to gaze moodily at a concealed photograph of your favourite! The second-born and so evidently the prettiest of the Dean's daughters.

'The child, Alice,' I said brusquely, lurching forward, and you started when I tapped your knee. Your oh-so-refined features looked pained.

'*Mann und Mädchen.* You're both so attuned you think as one. It must be a torment in the Long Vac to be denied her company.'

'True,' you conceded reluctantly, collecting yourself. 'The summer idleness of a bachelor in holy orders is a long and a sad tale.'

A gloating smile escaped my lips.

'Yet, *I*, on the other hand, as a private tutor with *no* stipendiary position . . . *I* am nowise so discountenanced for I see my own young pupil every day. '

I removed a crumpled portrait photograph from my pocketbook.

'May I present Miss Elise. Elise von Alpenberg is the only daughter of a merchant banker. She is nine years' old and has green eyes.'

'I see,' Oxford's morosest logician observed, 'yet some green-eyed little girls in my experience are bad tempered, and moreover it appears to me that all good-tempered little girls have eyes that are not green.'

A nerve beneath your right eye began to twitch.

'Yes,' I agreed without pause. 'But will you not also grant, *mein lieber Herr Professor*, that green-eyed little girls that are not well-fed are often unhappy. And many happy girls with eyes that are not green are well fed.'

'Is El-*li-li-li* ... ' you stammered. Then you drew yourself up, caught your breath, and asked sharply, 'Is *Elise* indeed underfed?'

'Like a little beggar-girl,' I grinned. 'She also has tooth-ache.'

'No pain is eagerly wished for,' answered the logician. 'All toothache is tiresome. All dentists are dreaded by children.'

'Little Miss Elise says all medicine is nasty.'

'Laudanum is a medicine,' countered the logician. 'Laudanum is not nasty.'

'The child is a riddle.'

'It's an irrefutable paradox that no riddles interest me that can be solved.'

'*Ach!* She is a riddle that is insoluble, *mein Freund.*'

'A beggar-girl, you say, yet an heiress?'

I nodded. 'No rich man begs in the streets, yet many old misers are thin.'

'True. And all improbable stories are doubted. *Argumentum ad lapidem.*'

'I *insist*. The child is pale and underfed. Are you are saying the circumstances of my tenure are not probable?'

'I did not say that. A prudent man shuns improbabilities. None but misers hoard eggshells. And no child who is not pale looks poetical. '

'The banker's daughter is pale and sweet and looks poeti-cal.'

'No bankers write poetry and some sweet things are unwholesome.'

'And some clerical gentlemen are damned unreasonable! No argument can overwhelm the fact that she is *abandoned*. A child in need of solace. And no greater service could be ren-dered, my dear Dodgson, than your attendance at the Hall this Long Vacation.'

'I do-do not wish to enlarge on this matter,' you said breathlessly.

(Never was a weaker defence attempted than that presented by the Revd. Do-do-dodgson's disingenuous writhings! Never was there an instance of greater self-duplicity! Haha!)

'Very well,' I pressed on, 'then let me speak with the greatest care when I tell you that she is the most sublime specimen of girlhood you are ever likely to encounter.'

I placed my photo of Elise beside the photo of your Alice to compare. It must have struck you they were not dissimilar in age, for it was plain to see.

'The house is ours alone at weekends,' I continued winningly, 'so we shall not be disturbed. Just you, myself, Miss Elise and the deaf cook.'

'A deaf cook?'

(At that moment you failed, my dear sir, to conceal a furtive sign that your mood had brightened.)

'No house guest,' I said, 'could hope for domestic staff more discreet. There is none discreeter than a deaf cook with a dumb waiter in the basement ...'

'... *and both turning a blind eye to the basic tenets of decorum, I have no doubt,*' I heard you mutter.

'Come, sir,' I wheedled. I could see you were wavering. 'Tell me you agree to teach her for a spell. She rules, I promise you, an enchanted realm.'

'Unexplored countries are certainly fascinating,' the logician with a sigh belatedly allowed.

∿

AN UNEXPLORED COUNTRY.

You remember? How could you forget the first time you met her in the great drawing room? She was standing in front of a large claw-footed chair, which only served to draw greater attention to her extreme fragility.

She was wearing her nicest dress of silver-gilt gauzy stuff over powder blue sateen with the bodice defined by non-concentric circles in the form of tinsel trimming and beaded appliqué. She was toying with her sash.

'Dear child,' you said with a gracious bow, 'you really can have no notion of how delighted I am to be your guest. I feel most keenly the honour. And may I say you are most splendidly dressed for an occasion that surely does not warrant such ceremony.'

This was not an encouraging opening for a conversation but Elise replied, rather shyly, in her tender little voice, 'Indeed, sir, I . . . I . . . I hardly know why this is the case. I cannot say what I wore this morning, but I think I must have changed several times since then.'

'At Halkerstone Hall,' I butted in, 'we change our clothes quite as often as we change our principles for fear of becoming dull. '

Elise indicated a seat for her guest, then took her place on the claw-footed chair with her silk-clad legs, extraordinarily perfect, outstretched before the fender. Although pale in complexion and thin as a whipping post, she was poised and upright in her comportment, yet apparently unaware that her charming little feet, tapping on the fireguard, had carried up her petticoats to reveal with that action her virginal slender ankles.

To suppress a tremor you made a sketchy motion with one hand in the direction of the window, the rose-beds and the parklands beyond.

'What could be more captivating than a weekend in the country,' you said, clearly unwilling to remove your gaze from hers. You paused as if you thought that somebody ought to speak, yet no one else seemed inclined to say anything.

So you sat silent and drank in her fragrance. Her camomile hairwash. Her half-formed girl-nature.

Her hands, you recall, smelled always of eucalyptus soap.

There was a rattle of a pulley, and the speaking tube whistled above the shaft of the dumbwaiter.

A tray of tea things was laid for three, and Elise helped you to some bread-and-butter. Your fingers moved in a hurried nervous manner.

'To crumble your bread, sir,' Elise said in a very respectful tone, but frowning, 'is proof I'm told of shyness. I do so, too, when in terror of failing my lessons.'

She crossed her hands on her lap as if she were attentive to her schooling.

'Come sit beside me and my guardian will play a lullaby to soothe us both. Beethoven.'

She moved to a sofa and patted a space beside her.

I took my place at the piano and played *Für Elise*.

'Do I look very pale?' I heard Elise ask in a low voice, turning to you as she spoke. 'Today I happen to have a toothache.'

'Take some more tea,' you advised very earnestly.

'I've had nothing yet,' Elise laughed, 'so I can't exactly take *more*. I suppose I ought to drink something or other for my woes, but the great question is: *what?*'

At these words, my rolling arpeggios tumbled to a lovesick dying fall and I joined you both on the sofa: two ardent Euclidean geometrists with their adored pupil between them; or, if you prefer, three parallel planes, perpendicular to the sofa, whose intersection had yet to be postulated.

The blue glass bottle of Laudanum I then produced from my pocket I placed on the tea tray beside three sherry glasses.

'Adults, thirty drops,' Elise recited, reading from the label.

'And ten-year-olds, fifteen drops,' you pronounced, 'if I am not mistaken.'

'I understand it is pleasant to drink,' I said, pouring three glasses of the finest manzanilla olorosa, 'though I have not yet ventured to taste it.'

Thereupon, I took a glass pipette and dispensed drops in each glass in accordance with the instructions.

'*For every one, we're given two.*' You commenced an impromptu chant like casting a spell. Evidently this rhymer's trick of enticement was one of your diversionary ploys. '*For every one, we're given two, or given three or more, there never was a stronger draught than that poured here-to-fore.*'

Elise seemed duly enchanted and I noticed, in consequence, you availed yourself of this gift by squeezing up closer to her side as you spoke.

'I can hardly breathe!' she protested crossly. 'You would think someone wanted to squeeze me flat! At least, I would not wish you to grow any larger.'

'I can't help it,' the rhymer said very meekly. 'But, indeed, it is *you* who are growing, child, if truth be told.'

'Well, I *do* hope to grow somewhat taller soon, for I fear I am really quite tired of being a child when growing up makes one's shins hurt so.'

'*Dolor sub incremento,* my dear,' I consoled her, 'you may be certain that bilateral aches in the long bones are unexceptional in a growing child of your years.'

She took up her glass again and very soon finished it off.

'The pain's going on rather better now,' she said in a low, trembling voice, and lightly passed her table-napkin over her lips.

'And your toothache?' You presumed to draw her attention to a deposit of her blood on the white linen crushed in her hand. You then added in an anxious tone, 'I hope no teeth are troubling you?'

'None to speak of. But, then, I often find a capital way *not* to remember unpleasant things is to shrink from thought altogether and do no more than wind my watch or simply brush my hair.'

'Then mayn't I brush it for you?' you proposed boldly, removing her hair brush from the pocket of her pinafore thrown over a chair. Your voice sounded hoarse and strange (a dry throat is often a consequence of Laudanum).

'Most girls' hair goes in long ringlets but mine doesn't go in ringlets at all,' Elise said very humbly.

Then she . . . then she . . . but, *wait*!

Is it not time, my dear Dodo, to hear these fervid impressions put into your own words! Because (dishonourable act!) did I not read and transcribe your diary that night as, overcome with Laudanum, in a sort of intoxication, you profoundly slept!

And what mischief I read! What indiscretions! What monstrous desires!

You surely cannot forget your first diary entry [Saturday June 27 1863] and your faithful description of myself (*too* scandalously candid!) and of the inordinate doings of the Revd. Dodo:

Our host, *in loco parentis*, seems to have a queer conception of the proprieties. His dark haggard face, arched eyebrows, hooked nose, gleaming teeth, strike the mind so forcibly that one could easily find one's self in thrall to him.

The potion felt quite strange at first but the Dodo got used to the changes within a few minutes.

Elise said, 'How queer everything is to-day! I almost think I cannot remember ever feeling so different. I am certainly not the same as I was when I got up this morning.'

The details on the panels of her dress below her collar bones reminded the Dodo of his lecture theatre and of the Apollonian

Circles he would describe on the blackboard, passing through two foci, A and B, and he was compelled to dwell on their orthogonal properties when she reached to retie the ribbon in her hair.

The Dodo could only think: *'How I would adore to see the radical axis redrawn the instant she raises her other arm.'* But the Dodo was to be sorely disappointed as that keen pleasure was denied. Even so, there remained for him a powerful desire to be permitted to trace a succession of intersecting lines in an elegant Euclidean construction to demonstrate the mutual tangency of the circles across her sternum and collar bone.

At the child's imperious instruction he had then brushed out her magnificent head of hair . . . out . . . out . . . as far and even farther than her charming pale arms extended!

The Infanta's flesh was of the most delicious creamy white, without spot or blemish, and dazzlingly fair and smooth.

And, after he had well brushed her crowning glory, she said with some severity, 'The brush has got entangled in it! Dear me, what a state my hair is in!'

Elise then carefully released the brush and did her best to get her hair into order, while prettily composing her kittenish mouth.

'But really you should have a lady's maid!' the Dodo heard his words falter.

'Take care,' von Thul whispered in his ear. 'Something's going to happen!'

The hair-brushing and the narcotic had evidently had their natural effect on the child's senses because, without her knowing why, she flushed suddenly and squeezed the Dodo tight against her person.

'Sometimes my growth is greater than I can bear,' she entreated in a piteous tone, almost ready to cry.

The child and the Dodo were now so close he could see an exquisite blue vein coursing down the otherwise flawless marble of her jaw. She was exactly the right height for him to rest his chin upon her shoulder.

Then Elise began to cry in earnest.

'Now, come, Elise, tell me all about it,' the Dodo said, putting his arm round the sobbing girl's child-girdled waist, and making her stand still closer beside him. 'There's surely nothing to cry about.'

'If it were nothing,' Elise said, half-laughing through her tears, 'I shouldn't be able to cry. The day may be hot but it has not made me stupid.'

'Then, it follows we may draw the logical inference from your remark that your recent growth is necessarily true. If only there were a precise corollary to demonstrate your previous size then we could find a formal proof easily enough.'

'But there *is*! Proof, I mean! I could show you that yesterday I was no more than a Thumbel ...'

'... a Thumbelina, a *Däumelinchen*,' von Thul cut in harshly, 'in comparison with which you'd call this child positively a *giantess*!'

Elise laid a hand upon the Dodo's arm and he held out his hand to hers.

Her hand was certain to be sweet to smell, the Dodo thought; and he longed to bend over it, and press it with his lips.

'Come here directly, sir,' she commanded, 'and get ready for a walk!'

Von Thul smiled mockingly upon them and opened the glazed double doors that gave on to the terrace.

The child led him into the loveliest garden he'd ever seen. The sunlit grounds were alive with bright flowers, and they followed a path across a croquet lawn, through a shrubbery into an orchard and hazelwood, and thence they came suddenly upon an open place to gain a little remote summer cabin in a clearing, fashioned in perfect miniature as a child-sized dollshouse.

The neat little house was about four feet to its ridge tiles and its little door was about fifteen inches high.

'Now we shall see!' exclaimed Elise eagerly, and those lips for kisses warm now pouted with childish vexation. 'Yesterday things went on just as usual, and I was quite small enough to get through the door; now it is as much as I can do to put my head into this poky little house, for I never was so grown as this before, *never*!

Suddenly, with all speed, she commenced to remove every particle of dress.

'I am so hot and giddy.'

Her silk dress was drawn up with care to prevent its being creased.

The Dodo found his desperately pinkening face pressed against her cool snowy white petticoats as she lifted her dress over her head, letting it fall to the path.

'Oh, I beg your pardon!' Elise exclaimed in a more subdued tone, and the Dodo, not daring to fully open his eyes, began picking up her undergarments as quickly as he could.

He felt her soft and dainty fingers as he handed them to her. The delicate perfume of young girlhood assailed his nerves.

When all but her chemise was removed, and her ivory shoulders were laid bare, she knelt down at the door to the little house.

Then, without warning, she spread out her hand, made a snatch in the air, and the filmy chemise lay at his feet.

She now wore nothing but her stockings, and tiny little slippers, fastened at the instep by bows, which, as she crawled on all fours across the threshold of the door, revealed little thin soles of rose-coloured silk.

'What a curious feeling!' Elise cried out from within. 'I am opening out like a telescope.'

The Dodo saw one arm appear out of the window, and the toe of one foot poked out of the chimney. He heard her muffled voice inside and stooped to listen.

'*Do* look! I'm a mile high!'

The Dodo thrust his head through the doorway and looked up into a tidy little room with a table under the window, and on it a Map of the World coloured no less pink than his own face.

'*T'would be the rash act of none but a fool,*' the Dodo repeated to himself in a whisper, '*to question the title of this child to rule.*'

The girl had stretched herself up on tiptoe and, with utter grace, had arched her torso over the map so her shadow fell across a planar British empire that spanned seven continents.

'At least there's no room to grow up any more here,' he heard a languid voice pronounce through slightly parted lips, but from which lips came the voice he could not be sure.

'*If only,*' the geometrist thought, '*if only I could inhabit the map's two-dimensional Euclidean space, with my gaze on this angel-child set vector to plane, then it's certain there would be no earthly feeling to compare with that single sensation of concen-*'

trated bliss she'd summon to pulse in the torments of pleasure's ineffable throb.'

From this imposed angle, nonetheless, he could examine the secluded inscapes of her unformed thighs and armpits, the underswell of her lower lip, the delicately scooped philtrum beneath her perfect nose, the shadow of her neck so privily hollowed at the nape, the sternal incurves at her breast, the rose-pink interstices, and all those unblown blooms whose sweetest gleaming nectar lay hid from him behind the secretest wall.

'And as for those growing pains,' the voice went on more cheerfully. 'I was foolish to cry about them, do you not agree?'

She brushed away tears from her long lashes, as though she, too, like the logician, had reviewed certain arithmetical principles and had discovered the correct axiomatisation of his love.

'A stolen kiss now,' he thought, as if stung by a spasm, *'and the proof of the axiom will be complete.'*

Just then, the curtain fluttered and, as Alice snaked towards him, a shaft of sunlight fell full upon her . . .

∾

At which point in the narrative, my dear Dodo, I bellowed jocularly, 'Recollect, sir, your position as a dignitary of the church!' and hauled you by your coat-tails out of that tiny house of ill-fame, like a terrier from a vixen's earth! 'I am horrified beyond measure,' I added for good measure.

And do not imagine, sir, that your all-revealing slip-of-the-pen, when your diary of that special day alludes to your own 'Alice', was ever likely to escape my searching scrutiny!

It's a truism, is it not, that even the most gifted mathematician can be confounded by one fatal error!

Taking the facts by themselves, I regret the Dean will not be the only member of the faculty to blackball your deaconship should word reach him of your libertine spree at Halkerstone Hall.

Try to form a mental picture of your shame.

I do not think I put an impossible case when I state that I, too, face ruin with neither stipendiary tenure nor a penny between me and a loaded pistol, unless you can help me in my extremity.

You understand my difficulty.

My regret is intensified by the thought that I find myself in the position of importunate petitioner and, startling as this may appear to you, it is an unpalatable *fact* that a Promissory Note under your hand to the sum of 500 Thalers is our only way out of this fix.

Pray, sir, let me say I am indebted to you in anticipation.

Cordially,
your confidant and *Bruder in Christus,*
Kepler von Thul

P.S. And may I say your descriptions of myself (the fêted author of *Die Fledermauskinder!*) in your interminable Alice manuscript (I peeked!) likewise did not escape my eagle-eyed glare? Even your irreverent acrostic mocking my noble name was penetrated in a trice!

The Hatter shook his head mournfully: 'It was at the great concert given by the Queen of Hearts, and I had to sing nursery rhymes for the Queen and verses written by the **K** ing, **v** ery **o** ften **n** onsense:

> **T** winkle, twinkle, little bat!
> **H** ow I wonder what you're at!
> **U** p above the world you fly,
> **L** ike a tea-tray in the sky.'

P.P.S. To prevent further misapprehension, you'll be glad

to learn that little 'Miss Elise' counsels me to spare your feelings with her confession that you, as privileged repository of uncommon knowledge (*viz*. her state of dishabille), are not entirely unique. I may tell you now that nineteen-year-old Miss Kitty O'Moyne (petite, green-eyed *contorsionniste danseuse* and *fille de joie*) shed buckets of real tears after you departed. She was a 'jolly good sport' (as you English say) to enter into the spirit of the thing and to let herself be put up to the prank.

As willing *ingénue* in our playlet, she demonstrated a gift for improvisation that is a credit to her profession. Yet, there's a true pathos in the revelation that the rigours of a life *en pointe* keep some dancers in a perpetual state of prepubescence (a state, however, not undesirable to certain discerning patrons of our Miss Kitty).

As to her consumptive pallor, Miss Kitty tells me that the merest dab of mortician's powder can produce the impression she has quite fainted away! Indeed, she is a well-practised exponent in the art of extracting money from her male devotees by seeming to suffer from a tubercular cough! She dissimulates the blood in her sputum by pricking her gums with a pin!

Nota bene. The blinkered logician must take heed to the dangers of inferring causes from effects! *Fallacia consequentis!* Yours is as bad a case as could be demonstrated.

Postquam-Post-Scriptum: Warnung! Your failure to respond to my solicitations will compel me to seek another more willing correspondent for my salvation, namely Kaspar-Ulrich Markheim, the fabulously wealthy Viennese publisher and bibliophile of *Erotische Phantasien*. What he will make of the curdled pillow-problems and lascivious effusions of a sleepless Oxford don I cannot yet predict, tho', given your celebrity (or should I say 'infamy'), doubtless my *complete* transcription of your journal will fetch any price I choose to put upon it.

For additional explanatory *Notes* on Carroll's diary entry for Saturday June 27 1863, please refer to the final section of this book.

Filename: **Marthe Colvaine**
Classification: **Betrayal**

IN SEARCH OF THE FOURTH MAN

Our grief... Not knowing that our blunt
Ideals would find their whetstone, that our spirit
Would find its frontier on the Spanish front ...

The Hammer and Sickle was scrawled over Spain that
Easter.

Louis MacNeice, c.1936.

Dargee was probably the finest horse that ever walked at
Crabbet Stud...

Lewis Payne, American breeder of Arabians.

IN SEARCH OF THE
FOURTH MAN

'But s'pose I make a social hash of it and fail to recognise him?' I complained to my boss with mock petulance.

The directress of publicity at the Mayfair publishing house, where I worked as a junior copywriter, turned on me her keenest interrogatory society smile.

She had taken me under her wing and, because I admired her, I would often find myself unconsciously aping the lightness of her conversational mannerisms whilst fearing the deadly barbs of her polished wit. Indeed, to protect the memory of my mentor, I shall call her Barbara (not her real name). A barb-arrow. An arrow whose barb so frequently hit the mark.

'You'll recognise dear Tony, depend on it,' she purred.

Barbara was celebrated for anatomising our authors with deadly skill.

'Just look for a long face where all the colours have run like an indifferent watercolour abandoned by thieves in the rain.'

∼

We were seated in the bar of Brown's Hotel in Dover Street. Fortunately, the hotel was sited directly opposite our marketing offices in Ely House so Barbara, with ease, must have had many opportunities to rate her daiquiris until they were mixed to perfection. In those days there was a double bar, with two bar attendants, one an American who shook cocktails so frenziedly it appeared as though a sword had been put into a madman's hands.

Despite the smog that darkened the window, two magnificent coal fires blazing in the lounge conspired to intensify an atmosphere conducive to confidences.

'Marthe, take a look at this,' grinned Barbara slyly. She unsnapped her Chanel quilted handbag and withdrew a folded cutting.

'*This* has been going the rounds in the ladies' loos. That's Sir Anthony to the life.' She gave a throaty laugh.

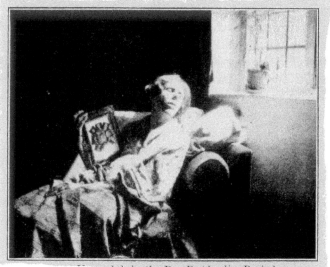

...in the Pre-Raphaelite Period.

I examined with astonishment the photograph of a figure

who resembled my late great-aunt, a craft weaver in the Outer Hebrides.

'He was always a bright boy,' Barbara continued almost tenderly. 'This was an undergraduate lark for *Granta* in the late nineteen-twenties.'

She returned the cutting to her bag.

'1929, to be precise. Forty years' ago, now I think of it. But ...*Rien n'est beau que le vrai!* He won't bite you! He's very good with children. My two scamps positively adore him.'

Barbara glanced at her watch with a start.

'Speaking of which, I must fly or the kiddies won't have their tea!' She thrust into my hands a proof copy of Sir Anthony Blunt's *Guernica* fresh off the press.

'Tony marked the item last night, but somehow I've lost the page. Simply ask him to confirm again the plate he wants for the publicity fliers.'

She drained the last of her glass, gathered her scarf and gloves, and, effortlessly *soignée* even in haste, she swept out without a backward glance.

～

I emerged from the hotel into a clammy smog dense enough to rival the 'fen-suck'd fogs' that still besiege Ely and Cambridge.

My decision to hike the goodish mile to the Courtauld Institute in Portman Square was conditioned by my neurotic avoidance of bus passengers in winter and their insufferable snuffling.

The task assigned to me by Barbara I regarded as a no less painful ordeal.

On the previous Monday we'd taken the packed rush-hour Varsity Pullman from Paddington to the press at Oxford.

Barbara and I had dined elbow-to-elbow with week-ending dons from the metropolis in a vintage breakfast-buffet car.

A querulous don had stabbed his *Times* crossword with his fish-knife and quavered, 'Male newlyweds are separated in Scottish islands, eight letters?'

'He-brides,' my sophisticated companion replied instantly and I thought then that I'd never measure up to the adaptive wit of Barbara. (I learned, years later, that her own marital status was something of a 'lavender marriage'.)

The dining car had a special brown and cream livery of faded elegance, I remember, with furnishings the colour of Oxford marmalade. Our hair when we arrived had smelled of roasted coffee, burnt toast and smoked kippers.

A desiccation of fusty-dusty dons!

For, when later that same morning we attended a marketing meeting convened by our own editorial board of dons in their Master's Lodge, we'd found ourselves again seated among a dozen ill-assorted ancient chairs similarly crammed into a book-strewn brown study.

The subfusc milieu of the Courtauld Institute I feared would be no different. The driest wits seem to sit at High Table or inhabit Senior Common Rooms.

In short, the most remarkable thing about Oxford dons I'd discovered at that time was, alike, they all struck me as quite *studiously* unremarkable.

Theirs was the slow, measured speech of the hind-sighted.

Each seemed to compete to be an Everyman, taking pride in speech of studied simplicity, the raw stuff of common idiom from which they'd refine their epigrammatic sallies.

'They do say you go into hospital with one thing and come out with another,' mused a wizened don, idly flipping the pages of a new *Vade-Mecum of Treatments for Pathological Conditions*.

'Duck shove it,' said another brusquely, consigning an unpublished manuscript to obscurity.

The meeting concluded with a discussion to decide the merits of a learned treatise on ceremonial banqueting in the Quattrocento.

'Is it illustrated?' a don asked, examining the prospectus through half-moon bi-focals.

'Regrettably, not,' Barbara answered.

'Dear me,' the don observed peevishly, 'then how are we to serve a good dinner without any *plates*?'

And *then* – at *that* precise moment – Anthony Blunt's incisive new study of Picasso's *Guernica* surfaced in error to the top of the stack.

'Mmm. Alas, poor Tony,' the elder of the discussants murmured with a strange little moue of discontent.

Sage heads nodded. And there was a knowingness in the general mutterings of reproach when the senior don added:

'He makes new friends as readily as he abandons old ones.'

So I fully expected my imminent encounter with Sir Anthony Blunt – a former Cambridge don, after all – to be likewise as dry and donnishly waggish.

$\sim$

THE OTHERS.

I heard lordly voices through the veneered door of the anteroom.

There was a museumy smell of paint varnish and wood oil.

'His prose was as perfumed as his pocket-handkerchief,' a man was saying in scholarly tones.

'In fact,' he continued with a stifled yawn, 'I've always professed a decided disrelish for Disraeli.'

The remark was greeted by neighing laughter and the chink of many glasses.

There are some people whose presence in a room seems to exert a disturbing centre of gravity around which lesser minds orbit, overawed by the oppressive dead weight of that attraction.

Such was the presence of Sir Anthony Blunt, KCVO, knight of the realm and Keeper of the Queen's Pictures.

I felt the colour mounting in my face. I had never quite overcome my fear of entering a strange drawing room, certain to be caught in the cross-beams of intense curiosity or, sometimes, outright suspicion.

I heard the voice – a mellifluous modulated drawl – continue.

'I was crossing the square this morning when I bumped into Eddie Portman. He told me the parking attendant had tried to give him a ticket.'

(A fluting voice, *sotto voce*, murmured reverentially: *'Tony must mean the ninth viscount.'*)

'The attendant flew at him in a passion and said, "D'you think you own the place?" and Eddie said, "Well, as matter of fact I do." '

(Prolonged laughter.)

Yes. I confess it. I still retain a dread of entering a room of social smiles but, on that occasion, hands shaking, I pushed the door and walked in.

∼

It is also true that – like many people who admit to an impressionable youth – I continue to carry through life a remembrance of certain words probably long forgotten by the speaker.

The Queen's *cavalier servente*, I remember, was standing in a commanding attitude by the French windows of his study on the first floor of the Institute.

A breeze had sprung up so he moved to close the half-open balcony window; the moon, I noticed, had broken through the fog.

I observed Sir Anthony surreptitiously beneath lowered lashes while I pretended to examine a small maquette on his desk, an ill-carved figure he evidently used as a paperweight among his card index boxes.

'One can see with half an eye it's a fake,' were Blunt's first words.

In his own eyes, I thought, there is nothing written he allows you to read.

They were eyes I deemed the palest Cambridge blue, set in the face, I guessed, of a jaded critic nothing could rouse.

There were wine bottles on the table and he poured me a glass. He had the slow dignity and well-brushed appearance of a courtier.

Full of courtliness, I thought, full of guile.

He selected a salted almond more by manner than desire, for he toyed with the thing – in a caressing motion of his fingers – while with ceremonious courtesy he asked where I was living in London. I told him I was temporarily quartered in a little bedsit near Kensington Gore.

'It's behind the Royal College of Art,' I said. 'Jay Mews.'

'*J'amuse les autres quelquefois aussi, ma jeune fille innocente,*' he laughed.

∼

That 'innocent young girl' has often wondered since whether Blunt, when he admitted to 'sometimes also amusing the others', attached a deeper meaning to *les autres*, all his own. Because, when I think of his words today, here at the dawn of the new millennium, I am reminded of the curious fact that our intimate conversation in the twentieth century was undoubtedly recorded by MI5 who, we now learn, had bugged Blunt's rooms with listening devices, concealed in the walls.

So, in the Records vaults of MI5, operatives in the secret services may still, if they choose, listen once more to the following exchanges:

'I have a message from Barbara,' I began.

'Ah! Barbara! If we didn't argue we wouldn't be friends.' He did not relax his half-bantering manner. He gazed at his guests with a certain tolerant contempt, lips pouting, expressive of a famished sexuality.

Women, I'd heard, found him gaunt but totally attractive. Certainly Barbara had admitted to, on occasion, going weak at the knees. Slim-waisted, sparely built, Blunt stood over six foot, yet his narrow shoulders sloped like a hock bottle's.

(It's true that according to the magisterial biography – *Anthony Blunt: His Lives* by Miranda Carter – Blunt's 'ascetic looks' were considered 'elusively desirable' by the opposite sex. Moreover, he's known to have had at least two love affairs with women.)

'Truth be told I no longer remember,' he countered wearily, as though the phrase was well-honed, when I asked him to identify the Picasso plate for his book. He denied any knowledge of his earlier choice and replaced the marker at a different page . . . a preparatory drawing for *Guernica*, a curious winged creature that, as Blunt states in his monograph, flies out of a wound in the flank of a tormented horse, and 'symbolises the soul of the horse, which leaves it at the moment of death.'

'I adore Arab horses,' Blunt said. 'My Uncle Wilfrid bred them.'

'He did *not*,' I blurted out, without thinking.

'*Not?*'

There was a collective gasp, then awestruck silence.

The fawning young men had ceased haw-hawing around him. They were much as I'd imagined them; the sort of men, I thought, that would be sure to detect a run in the blue stocking of any woman who presumed to contradict them.

I drew a breath then spoke all in a rush: 'As I recall, his horses were bred by one man alone, and *his* name was *George Ruxton*. Lady Wentworth told me herself that without George she'd never have owned the finest Arabian bloodline in Europe since . . . (I gulped and there were sounds of stifled snickering) . . . since . . . well, since Bucephalus. Wasn't Lady Wentworth your uncle's daughter?'

There followed an abrupt transition from feigned indifference to a quite different playfulness of tone.

'She was indeed,' Blunt said with an affable, almost conciliating air. 'You have no need to borrow confidence, *Kamarad*, because you're perfectly right. Old George was one of a kind.'

The narrow cadaverous face broadened with a smile as he continued:

'A hunter groom at the Royal Show once pointed him out. The groom said, "See that bloke over there? Well, he breeds the best Arabs in the land and never pays more'n twenty-five pounds for any of 'em." It was George, leading an Arab with the red ribbons up, his favourite ... '

'*Dargee!*' we exclaimed as one.

(The champion, Dargee, was the most famous stallion of Ruxton's in the Crabbet Stud.)

Blunt took a sip of wine and his nose wrinkled. That acidic downcast mouth reminded me of a turbot with a lemon slice in it.

'The wine is drawn, it must be drunk,' he observed sorrowfully.

We were drinking a four-year-old Château Mouton Rothschild and it tasted of rotten mushrooms. The label of naked dancing Bacchantes, I later learned, was designed by a noted Surrealist painter and sculptress, which was distinctly odd since Blunt's biographer tells us that he abhorred *le Surréalisme* (or 'Superrealism', as he referred to it) and, besides, that Bordeaux we drank that night was one of the worst vintages of the last two centuries.

In my ignorance I did not dare betray my distaste. One error can breed more, I thought, so I remained silent. Sometimes – even though a foulness may linger on the palate – the greatest virtue is to hold one's tongue.

To mask my action while disposing of my own glass on a mantleshelf, I examined more closely a Picasso *Femme Assise* hanging on the chimney-breast, an exquisite pen and ink drawing.

'It'll cost you the thick edge of a hundred grand,' Blunt said harshly as he turned away, withdrawing once more into his lofty solitude.

'It's simply marvelous,' I said, but I could see I was preaching to the choir.

He spread out his hands and shrugged. A tic began to twitch

on his right cheek. Those downcast disappointed lips were no doubt a judgement on the jejunity of my utterances in a world where trust made way for treachery and where there was no place for my unworldliness.

Below the mantle, I noticed, on the chimney-piece, a *relievo* winged Cupid, reflected in a mirror, appeared to direct Love's darts aimlessly through the window in the general direction of the garden in the square, where the dappled bark of the plane trees glowed in the dark.

～

My heels clicked on the marble floor of the entrance hall. Someone had hung my coat on a hat-stand under the lamp and, as I retrieved it, I noticed the walls were painted imitation marbling up to the cornices.

'We see least with borrowed eyes,' my art mistress once said with emphatic earnestness in my last term at school, and I'd vowed then to always question the witness of my own sight.

For I remember clearly with no false memory that sour wine evening at the Courtauld, and Blunt's magniloquent diction as he turned on a guest his frigid disdain. A pretty young man had dared to revive the subject of Disraeli's ambivalent sexuality.

Blunt broke off with a scornful laugh and, smoothing a wing of hair, said:

'Call it what you will, but I have only one belief and that's an extraordinarily strong one: better your left hand should never know what your right hand is doing.'

Blunt then made a slicing gesture with his hands symbolic of quittance from a subject distasteful to him.

And I thought then – all those years ago before his fall – when discreetly observing, in the mirror of his study, the disengaged air of that pale and bloodless man . . . I thought then there was something in the movement of his high-held head suggestive of a more complex character than the society figure who hitherto had been just a passing mention in the bland pabulum of the Press.

As Barbara had exclaimed when, long afterwards, the scandal broke and she read of Blunt's confession in the newspapers:

'Dear old baffling Tony. Less a refusenik, more of an excuse-nik.'

A remark which sort of reflected, I thought, Blunt's love of schoolboy puns.

(His schoolchum and best friend was the poet Louis Mac-Neice whose shared love of puns is evidenced in the epigraph I've prefixed to these otherwise rather ungarnished, prosaic reminiscences of mine. *'Not knowing that our blunt ideals would find their whetstone* ... ' seems to allude more to Blunt's conversion to Marxism than to stand simply as a keepsake of their travels together in republican Spain during Easter 1936.)

At the time of Blunt's disgrace, Barbara was typing her own memoirs and her upper lip, I remember, was permanently stained from the purplish-blue carbon flimsies.

Never before had I seen her face so smudged and careworn, and it seemed to mirror my own sense of whirling confusion as though we were both marked by a stain; and, even today, like a wine-stain to white linen my old distrust still clings.

∾

In actuality, I still have that proof copy of Blunt's monograph, *Picasso's Guernica*. The label states:

UNCORRECTED ADVANCE PROOF COPY
NOT FOR RESALE

Between pages 30 and 31 is tucked a redemption card from a game of *Monopoly* to mark the place. Clearly, 'Uncle' Tony had been amusing Barbara's children on the afternoon preceding my interview with the great man. Even today I continue to suspect a deeper complicity in his friendship with Barbara, and can't be sure whether his nonchalant gamesmanship in playing that card is evidence of their sharing a private joke.

A number of Blunt's adoring women friends were suspected by MI5 of acting as couriers to relay messages within the Cambridge spy ring, so I wonder whether Barbara was alerted, too, by a keen throb of significance when she saw that winged prisoner flying free of his cage, the counterpart to the winged soul of the horse, which so clearly prompts Blunt's empathy as an escapee from oppression.

Remember, when we met that evening in the Courtauld, Blunt was enjoying immunity from prosecution as the price of his confession to MI5 five years earlier, a fact kept hidden from the nation; and his weary, *'Truth be told I no longer remember,'* was most likely the stone-walling response of a man who was subjected to regular intense interrogations to extract full disclosure of his treachery.

The strain was so great on the spy during all those years

of MI5 debriefings that for more than two decades Blunt was regularly prescribed Seconal as a tranquillizer.

Hardly surprising, then, that the man who'd endangered the lives of one hundred and seventy-five thousand Allied servicemen, by betraying the secret of the D-Day landings to his Soviet masters, must have feared his days were numbered.

The higher a man rises the greater his fall.

Blunt's covert reference to *'pour encourager les autres'* I now realise might well have been his own intimation of the punishment the Establishment demanded for his betrayal, a sentence of ignominy that would never be commuted . . . the ultimate sanction . . . to be stripped of his knighthood and removed as an Honorary Fellow of Trinity College, Cambridge.

No, I could not have guessed then, when Sir Anthony walked me down the grand staircase that evening at the Courtauld Institute in Portman Square – one of the finest examples of an eighteenth century unsupported staircase in Europe – that the mission of this pallid ultra-fastidious aesthete had been all along to knock away the underpinnings of the security of the West.

∽

AN UNREPENTANT SMILE.

These strange thoughts of those unforgotten years shimmered through me the other day when I strayed from Oxford Street to retrace my steps up Orchard Street to Portman Square. (There'd been a splendid sales offer of real linen sheets at Selfridges I'd been powerless to resist.)

The square as I remembered it was of a different epoch, a memory of an olive greyness, the London skyline still gap-toothed with bomb sites.

Now, new imposing cast-iron railings enclosed the square garden, a feature absent on that evening at the Courtauld when the little unfenced park had seemed abandoned and overgrown.

A leafy corner of Portman Square had been the fortnightly rendezvous point for passing classified military intelligence to Blunt from one of his spies working on the decrypted Enigma signals GCHQ had codenamed Ultra.

To tell the truth, I'd always fancied that a particular hollow tree, memorable for an eerie convolution of Arthur Rack-hamesque goblin faces swirling within its boles, had been Blunt's dead letter box *à la Russe.*

But now, alas, not a trace was to be seen.

The Courtauld Institute, of course, is also long ago departed from the square yet that magnificent palatial Adam mansion remains, once the private fiefdom, home, and seemingly unas-sailable position of the Fourth Man.

More ironies are seen to abound in the double life of Blunt when you pause to consider that this austere grandson of a C of E bishop, constrained by his crypto-commu-socialist aes-thetic, lived like a duke in a sort of doge's palace.

How emblematic of a man who could with such ease switch ideological hobby horses mid-stream, as it were, and serve simultaneously as a spy for Communist Russia and as a loyal liegeman of HM The Queen.

∿

Knight or knave? Friend or foe? That visionary dreamer, the poet Robert Graves, attempts to demystify this quidda-tive conundrum when defining the distinction between good poetry and fake poetry.

'When is a fake not a fake?' Graves asks.

Answer: 'When the lapse of time has obscured the original sources . . . and when the faker is so competent . . . that even the incorruptible porter at Parnassus winks and says "Pass, friend!" This sort of hermit-crab, secure in stolen armour, becomes a very terror among simple whelks.'

~

Well, I am unashamed to report that most of my life has been spent in the company of 'simple whelks' and among horsey folk who've mostly taken a Munnings-like view of Picasso and who are blind to any art but the canvases of *plein air* equestrian painters.

That robust sensibility of the Houyhnhnm, to whom deception is unknown, was demonstrated to me in my girlhood on the one occasion I met the 'Arab horsemaster', George Ruxton, down on his ten acres of paddocks in the heart of Hampshire.

He was then in his seventies and still in the saddle, hunting regularly with the vigour of a man half a century younger.

A farrier-sergeant in the Army Veterinary Corps, Ruxton had served in WW1 with my maternal grandfather, who'd introduced us.

I remember we were all three standing by the gate to a large outdoor equitation arena padded underfoot with sawdust, sand and bark shavings; Ruxton at that time was host to an informal riding academy.

Superb Arab ponies with wild manes outrivalling Delacroixian romanticism pawed the sand with tails flying like pennants.

When Grandpapa mentioned I was planning to go to art college, Ruxton winked and with a cutting laugh pointed to a sign on the riding school gate:

WHEN LEAVING THE SCHOOL
PLEASE TAKE YOUR DROPPINGS WITH YOU.

Both men had campaigned together and endured appalling privations. Clean drinking water had been a precious commodity and a soldier was under orders to water his horse first before he quenched his own thirst.

Grandpapa and Ruxton had served under the same colonel through three theatres of war. During all that time Grandpapa had outranked him.

As he reminded Ruxton, as he took his old friend's arm, water had been so scarce that Ruxton had been 'fourth man in line for the colonel's bathwater.'

How those two doughty old campaigners had laughed!

$\sim$

In that late afternoon of the January sales, these shadows of reviving memory seemed to compel my steps to return for one last nostalgic stroll around Mayfair, and I found myself again in Dover Street.

But when I saw once more the engraved mitre above my old offices at Ely House I was assailed by tormenting thoughts. How strange, I mused, that this ancient former palace of the Bishops of Cambridgeshire – and once home to Oxford's academic printers – should have published the Cambridge spy whose works would be forever associated with his irrevocably lost good name.

How, curious too – even romantic – that old George Ruxton had bred horses for the great-granddaughter of Lady Byron ... the widow of the poet had resided just a few doors down from Brown's Hotel where my journey had begun all those years before.

$\sim$

The sky above Mayfair was stained with purple and the

moon was rising though a mist as I pushed open the big brass-bound swing doors at the entrance to the hotel.

Had my zigzagging path to recover dark memories brought me any closer to an understanding of Blunt's over-ruling motives, I brooded; had anything truly changed? Had I come all this way to know no more?

The coal fires were still blazing, I noted, but on closer inspection I saw they were fakes and obviously gas-heated due to London's smoke abatement bye-laws.

Still, the lounge was as warm and welcoming as I remembered, and I was just on the point of removing my coat when a familiar figure entered the hotel and approached the bar.

My childhood friend Jocelyn!

That certain effeminate grace was unmistakable; he was wearing Grecian sandals and his blonded highlights quite clearly needed repair.

~

A quick word about Jocelyn. As an infant, Josey shrank from muscular sports and would play quite docilely for hours, changing the dresses of my doll, Thumbelinda.

Josey would flit around me – sedulously matching his steps to mine in a girlish gait – and I recall my mother's prescient words on the occasion of the birth of Jocelyn's younger sister when he was aged six .

Josey and I had been playing at the far end of a meadow. We'd made a table of fresh silage bales and on them Josey had, with precocious artistry, arranged chipped dishes of rose hips and old fishpaste pots filled with blue harebells, periwinkles and wild garlic. At the table, on the grass, he'd seated Thumbelinda.

Then we'd heard the deep fretful bellowing of Josey's father calling him from the far side of the hedge.

At his angry commands, I recall, we'd run so fast that my calves were chafed into wheals by the rims of my rubber gumboots.

In my haste I forgot Thumbelinda; and when I returned to the mown field the next day she and the grass-bales were gone.

I remember my bewilderment at my loss, and my confused envy when I learned Josey's mother had been delivered of another doll-like creature with whom I guessed he would soon be also besotted.

When my own mother took my hand and led me home she tried to explain the darker significance of that birth.

'Well, one daughter was enough, I should've thought,' she declared, shaking her head sorrowfully, 'but two daughters with a doting mother, what an agony for the father!'

It's a sinister fact that, even today, Jocelyn – an only son – never calls his only sister Joan anything but 'Yoni', and – perhaps resentfully – he never permits her to forget this underlying sexual innuendo.

∽

These thoughts occupied the forefront of my mind as I approached the hotel bar.

When I touched Josey on the shoulder, he started.

'Guilty conscience?' I murmured, bussing him on both cheeks.

'Well, as a matter of fact, yes,' he said with mock gravity. 'I've been meaning to tell you for simply yonks now.'

Josey grinned shiftily.

'*I stole Thumbelinda.*'

∽

If you enter the St. George's Bar in Brown's Hotel you'll be impressed by the brilliantly illuminated stained glass window that dominates the room.

The legend on the scroll reads *Saint George for England*.

When we were very little, Jocelyn and I were taken to see the Christmas production of *Where the Rainbow Ends* staged in London by the Italia Conti theatre school.

The play is the perilous journey of two children through the Dragon Country where they are rescued by Saint George from the clutches of the Dragon King.

Seated in the bright-lit cozy bar, while Jocelyn withdrew to order more drinks, I felt my throat suddenly tighten with a sense of betrayal, and I shivered as it was borne in upon me that there was now no Saint George to guard us on our quest to find where the rainbow ends . . . nor had there ever been.

I remembered the Fourth Spy who'd masqueraded in the stolen armour of a patriot.

I remembered his frozen cynical unrepentant smile.

And, as I gazed on the brightly lit panel of Saint George spurring his charger, and on the face of Jocelyn radiantly transformed by kaleidoscopic splinters of light, I meditated further on this neat refutation of a dream and on the astonishing variousnesses of Englishness one could encounter in London on a January day when the Continent is cut off by fog.

Filename: **'Barbara Ely'**
Classification: **Counterespionage**

INDUCEMENT

'Who needs a *nom de guerre* when a spy's best cover is her own birth certificate?'

'If one attempt in fifty is successful [for recruitment], your efforts won't have been wasted.'
KGB spy Kim Philby

INDUCEMENT

It was three o'clock in the afternoon of a sunless day last October when I entered the lobby of an unmarked building said to be the whereabouts of the Faucon Detective Agency. I could smell the coming rain in the air.

I was wearing my new evening coat, and a cocktail dress with a matching jacket patterned with dark blue clocks whose hands pointed to five-to-midnight.

I was neat, immaculately made up for the evening, but unperfumed. I was everything the well-dressed young wife of a successful barrister ought to be.

Yet I was terrified.

On the second floor, the tiled corridor led me, as I was instructed, to Suite 2F, where I paused in some confusion. And I was still staring with dread at the frosted office door when it opened and a tall, slender man, with a military bearing, stepped out and shook my hand.

'Edward Faucon,' he said. A taut smile. 'And you must be Constance Bryde.'

~

We sat on large hard chairs in the middle of that sparsely furnished office while Faucon prepared to record in his daybook the details of my case.

'We make no judgements here. We are not judges of the married state, nor . . . ' and here he regarded me with another shrewd smile ' . . . nor are we its *advocates*.'

His pen was poised, his manner as blank and receptive as the empty page.

'So . . . ?' He nodded.

I snapped open my evening bag on his desk and withdrew a handkerchief.

'It's the old, old story, I'm afraid, and I'm sure I'm not the first to find myself in a tight corner, expecting somehow to be granted peace of mind.'

I twisted and untwisted the handkerchief until the hems frayed.

'I'm no angel. You've heard it all before. Lonely, neglected wife. Remote, ambitious husband. A desperate affaire. Now I'm terrified my husband is having me followed.'

'Have you any evidence of this?'

'Instinct. No more. A feeling I'm always watched. Strangers who pass in the street and *seem* to look at me with a questioning air. But I have to be sure.'

Faucon noted the details of my regular rendezvous with Stefan . . . Tuesday and Thursday evenings, when Simon dined at his club in St James's.

Faucon glanced at his watch.

'We'll commence tomorrow. I'll show you the way out, backstairs.'

~

Extraordinarily enough, the previous day Simon had arrived at the Old Bailey without his wig-tin, a calamitous event in a routine as devoutly regulated as his.

In answer to a 'phone call from his clerk of chambers,

I took a cab up to Newgate. Inscribed on the battered box were the gilded letters, S.T. Bryde Esq., the very same initials of his sainted father, a high court judge. Indeed, inside that box reposed a begrimed horsehair wig that had once been his father's, presented to Simon by his mother after he'd completed his pupillage.

Outside the robing room, a flustered junior counsel appeared and peremptorily relieved me of my burden.

There is a gloomy retreat for refreshments, with private booths for silks, in an anteroom adjoining the barristers' quarters, so I took refuge at a table with a glass of lemon tea.

That's where Verity found me, sickened and glum in the chastened mood that afflicts all principled, unfaithful wives when their evasions weigh most heavily on them.

'What's eating you?' she demanded. 'No smile for your friend in court?'

Verity is a successful divorce lawyer from rival chambers who also defends criminal cases. We'd first met at an Inns of Court Ball.

'*Cherchez l'homme!*' she continued brightly. 'It's written all over your face.'

'I'd like to say you're wrong,' I sighed, 'but, if I'm an open book, I would not care for my husband to read it.'

'Then it is a *man!*' Verity grinned in triumph. '*Do* tell. I swear anything you say has the seal of the confessional.'

I looked searchingly into Verity's clever, speculative eyes and decided to tell her something of my dilemma . . . my reckless infatuation with Stefan, the circumstances of our first meeting, and my suspicions that we were under surveillance by private investigators, set on our trail at the bidding of a virtuous husband. (Like his father before him, thanks to those wig-box initials, Simon had, by familial association, assumed in legal circles the sanctity of a saint.)

'Stefan Kazimirov, you say?' Verity wrote my lover's name on a paper napkin. 'Mmm. I'll consult my little black book. I think there could be someone discreet enough to help. Now, don't brood, darling . . . give me a couple of hours, and I'll call you with a *name*.'

She regarded me quizzically.

'Seems to me, so far, only one person's hurt here, and that's *you*.'

Before noon, true to her word, Verity rang with a number that directed me to Faucon.

~

QUICK CHANGE RUSES.

'You must not worry yourself about this,' Stefan had replied calmly when I'd first proposed hiring a private investigator to test my belief that someone was tracking our movements and jotting them down in a secret report.

We were drinking cocktails at *Maxie's*. Honey Dew Screwdrivers. Vodka, Orange Juice and Melon Liqueur.

It was a Thursday, our tenth clandestine meeting, and my jitteriness had grown tenfold. On each occasion, I'd heeded Stefan's warning to alter my approaches to his apartment, and even to change cabs and double back on my route or take a detour should I sense professional snoopers on my tail.

He bought me an expensive reversible woollen coat – white bouclé on one side and camel wool flannel on the other – and proposed I should also alternate my footwear: high heels one evening, and loafers the next as, according to Stefan, these quick-change ruses could confuse a surveillance team long enough for them to lose their target in a crowded street.

Even my adding a hairpiece or unpinning my hair were tricks advised to evade recognition.

'You must break the regular patterns of your daily life,' Stefan decreed.

Yet he laughed uneasily when I continued to insist on engaging an enquiry agent to tail my putative stalker.

'Counter-surveillance! Think of the expense! Absurd!'

He fidgeted with his glass; it was clear he was rattled. 'If we're followed at all, it's more likely by my bosses from the export *byuro*, figuring how I'm overspending their budget!' Stefan is a geologist, and sub-section chief at his trade mission, trusted with the export of mineral commodities.

He laughed again, rather testily, with a little flicker of one eyelid to the barman, and called for another glass.

'We have more to fear from my masters than from your husband!' There was a hard irony in his voice. 'Disappoint them and they have a way of making their displeasure known.' He paused to consider for a moment. '*Suspicion* is their nature ... *unforgiving* ... and more vengeful than demons. Our commissars are quick to punish those who betray their trust.'

There was a look of dulled pain in his eyes, I thought, and I shivered.

'*Idiotizm!*' he suddenly burst out. '*Very well, then!* Why not a private enquiry of our own? *You* would be consoled at last ... while *I* would have proof that my private life, too, is beyond suspicion.'

He raised his glass, with a peculiar little twist of the lips as if he had made a mistake.

'Such a verdict would go some way, perhaps, to restoring that certain *insouciance* the *corps diplomatique* expects of me!'

$\approx$

Stefan's apartment was a bachelor's suite in Chesterfield House, Mayfair W1.

From his bullet-proof windows we could see beyond South Audley Street to Park Lane and the tree-lined walks that led to Rotten Row. We were a short stroll from the Dorchester.

On my first visit to the flat I had been astounded by such opulence, and Stefan had quickly pounced to reprove the *'idiotizm'* of my false assumptions.

'These rooms once belonged to an enemy of the state, a pampered minister-in-exile,' he jeered. 'Should we not then have restitution of what is ours by right? This property is the people's, and not a salon for parasites leeching on the running dogs of the West.'

'In *this* country,' I retorted, with visions of a similar forfeiture of our imposing terrace in Brunswick Gardens, 'property is our only hedge against economic mayhem, or so Simon says.'

'Tfu! The realpolitik of the plutocracy!'

Intense memories of that first tender afternoon together reawakened, as I changed into the day clothes I'd wedged into one side of his wardrobe, an outfit of the neutral beiges deemed by Stefan as sufficiently non-descript: one of several evasion tactics commended to defeat our nameless shadowers.

Stefan leant over me and kissed my neck as he withdrew from an upper shelf a neatly wrapped package bound by crisp silk ribbons.

'Open it.' His smiling dark eyes were bright and steady and once again I understood his singular power to make a woman happy.

I rustled inside to find a tissue-wrapped Gucci handbag.

'Well,' he asked in a low voice, 'are you pleased with it?'

'It's simply splendid,' I breathed, I was so taken aback.

Stefan unsnapped the catch, and pointed to a tiny eyelet in the moiré silk lining.

'A pinhole microphone.' He touched a concealed switch.

'It's simply splendid,' my voice echoed tinnily from a hidden speaker.

I was at a loss for words.

'I don't understand.'

'I'm sorry.' Stefan looked away uneasily. 'I regret I cannot, personally, act for you in this matter. A consultation with a private enquiry agent, the tool of your absurd divorce courts, is no place for me! Yet, if *I* am right and *you* are wrong, the *recorded* testimony of your tame detective could provide me with a first class intelligence report to outfox my masters.'

He shrugged. 'I have many rivals in my section who'd like to see me damned. If I am to come to grief, at least let me have the chance of knowing my enemy.'

His mistrust infuriated me. At once I protested fiercely that I would report faithfully all that any investigation disclosed, unencumbered by his furtive bugging gizmos.

'I *insist*. The wise general conquers his enemy by foreknowledge. I would not ask this of you unless I also feared for your own wellbeing. My masters can destroy us both with as little thought for you as for me.'

With trembling fingers I continued to dress. Stefan seemed always to have the final word.

≈

A COMBUSTIBLE MIXTURE.

'Alone? This cannot be true.' Those were Stefan's first words in that crush bar when he approached me unannounced at the end of the concert interval.

Yes. That was the fateful beginning of our affaire in June.

It was the perfect atmosphere, you might say, for a combustible mixture to react, when your two active components happen to be an Englishwoman alone at a bar stool, toying fretfully with an empty glass, surprised by an imposing man in correct evening dress distinguished by the insignia of several foreign decorations pinned to his chest.

'Allow me.' His briefest nod to the barman was magically productive of two more glasses.

It was smoothly done, yet somehow in the cadences of that exotic voice his overtures were not corny.

I smiled. His air of calm possession of the moment impressed me.

'I should be here with a friend,' I explained. 'But she's not shown up.'

I was puzzled. It had been a strange whim of Verity's to press on me a prized ticket to the front stalls and altogether out of character not to meet me in the foyer as planned.

'In my youth,' the stranger continued, indicating my concert programme, 'such works were forbidden.'

The word, 'forbidden', throbbed in my veins and I caught my breath.

The performance that evening had included Shostakovich's frenetic Piano Trio No.2 and his tragic Eighth Symphony, both banned when first composed.

'Yes,' I ventured, 'it's easy to imagine the critics would hear only what they were trained to hear.'

'Exactly!' He gave a deep curt laugh, not entirely pleasant, and shot me a keen glance. 'Even today, for us it is the case that the less you know, the more soundly you sleep.'

How I wish I had heeded those words, for I would not now be condemned to the troubled sleeplessness that is my curse.

∾

'Are we happy?' I asked early one evening, not long after we'd first met.

Stefan had risen from the disarray of the bed to pad to his dressing room in search of his robe.

I stretched my arms wide in mock entreaty, willing him to answer. He paused and allowed one hand to linger on my knee.

His answer was as gnomic as it was quaint in its rusticity.

'As happy,' he murmured, 'as two flies in a dark forest that bask on a sunlit leaf.'

I saw a sudden hardening of his face.

(*'And the duration of our love,'* I told myself, *'is sure to be no longer than the lifespan of those flies.'*)

With a quick, impatient, interrogative glance, his mood shifted. He opened the wardrobe, selected a modest calf-length skirt with a waisted jacket, and flung them on the bed.

'Stir yourself. It's time to dress. An informal export meeting is to be convened directly, and the honour of your gracious presence is requested.'

'Me? I know nothing of foreign trade!' I slipped into the skirt.

'*Élegantnyi!* I cannot imagine how we have ever managed without you.'

He handed me my hairbrush.

'No perfume,' he warned. 'We need a blank canvas. I wear no aftershave. Remember. When a person is nervous their scent reacts to their body heat.'

～

A few paces down Stanhope Gate and we stood in the lobby of the Dorchester.

Again I felt there were a hundred eyes watching me, so conspicuous did I feel among the haut monde in the drab guise Stefan had insisted I assume as his private *sekretar*.

However, Stefan took in my appearance approvingly.

'There is no mystery as to your attendance at this meeting,' he confided. 'Essentially, you are here as the conjuror's assistant to sustain an air of delicacy and demure rectitude, while I act for the greater interests of our plenipotentiary overlords.'

He then initiated me into various secret signs I was to recognise during his negotiations. For instance, should he adjust the knot of his necktie or tug his earlobe when he presented me with a draft treaty, I was simply to shake my head sorrowfully and say, *'Nel'zya.* Impossible.'

∼

On entering one of the hotel's grandest drawing rooms overlooking Mayfair, I was immediately struck by a sense of having been transported to the Levant, for it seemed I was led into the belly of a vast, blindingly white, silk pavilion.

And, indeed, judged by the rich carpets and tapestry hangings, the huge room had been designedly transformed into the sort of ceremonial tent in which visiting emissaries find themselves when tribal elders hold court.

Stefan, evidently without hesitation, picked out the ruling mind in that room, because he at once approached a dark, sombre man, standing alone, cloaked in the purest white linen. I had a quick impression of a short black beard and of a warrior nose with a crescent-like curve; yet, puzzlingly, the mouth was parted slack, while a pair of dulled black eyes, shaded by the immaculate linen headpiece, gazed on the room with a dreamy detachment.

I was shown a seat at the outermost margin of the negotiating table, and sat, as instructed, with submissive bowed head.

Of those negotiations I remember only the endless salaaming and cups of sweet tea, with Stefan responding in a conciliatory low murmur to the urgings of a vizier until, apparently with reluctance, my lover unclipped his gold pencil and wrote a number of figures on a document placed before him.

'We know the weakness of your position.'

A suave voice from beneath the headpiece sounded for the first time.

The vizier folded the paper and tore it into any number of scraps.

'Agreed,' Stefan accepted smoothly. 'And I know the strength of yours.' (Did I detect a hint of irony in his words?)

Stefan again wrote the figures and brought the paper to where I was seated.

He adjusted his necktie.

'Nel'zya.' I grimly shook my head. 'Impossible.'

Before he snatched away the paper, I glimpsed a smattering of terms from the procurement contract held in contention: '... *certified issue of one-kilogram platinum ingots ... said price per troy ounce, pursuant to the provisions of State Repository bullion statutes.*'

In Stefan's game of bluff it was not until the conjuror's assistant had twice repeated her rehearsed denials that a deal was struck.

This consummate stagecraft saw the conjuror rewarded with an elephant-hide attaché case packed tight with dollar bills.

Within minutes we stood once more in the sunshine of Park Lane.

Stefan tightened his grip on the case to take my arm.

'Something on account,' he grinned. 'A *pourboire* for the messenger.'

He tapped the underside of his nose in a manner suggestive of his next remark.

'Did you not notice? Our bartering was more than usually favoured by the attentions of a *kokainist* as our presiding host.'

I did not smile.

More than ever I felt there were eyes fixed upon us, from every corner watching each gesture, each change of expression, every slip.

$\sim$

If I had dared to hope I could steal home that evening unobserved, I was to be summarily disappointed.

Our housekeeper opened the door before my key was in the latch.

Jealous eyes glowered at me, then a look of cunning betrayed her tireless zeal to admonish.

'Ye'll be wantin' a bath.'

Since my marriage I had learned her fierce defensiveness could not be gainsaid, but I did not let her see me wince.

From my husband's earliest infancy, he and Nannie Wicklow, if she was to be believed, had never once passed a single day apart.

She still smelled of the Creamola rice custard she prepared each day to satisfy Simon's nursery-tea palate.

As she retreated to the kitchen, fingers agitated on her apron strings, she turned to look searchingly over her shoulder as if seeking another pretext to wound.

I heard her mutter, *'Forgitting herself, the feeble craiture! A saucy hoor so she is.'*

She slammed the kitchen door but it could not muffle her next passionate outburst.

'Wull ye not gi' up your evil ways an' repent an' crave the church's pardon, on your knees?'

Why, I thought, was there this ill-considered imperative to appoint an enquiry agent, when Nannie Wicklow was so eminently qualified in the art of ferreting out my transgressions.

∾

On the first floor, our bedroom was separated from the bathroom by Simon's study – a cell-like space in no way made beautiful by its walls lined by long rows of legal volumes on shelves that covered every surface. A desk light glowed on the unfolded evening paper Nannie Wicklow, by custom, made ready for her master, and I stopped short on the threshold.

SPY CASE: 'SECRETS ACT BREACHED BY ROGUE CODE BOFFIN'

Today, Simon Bryde QC, prosecuting, in his preliminary arguments, told the packed courtroom: 'This case involves a clear-cut breach of Section One of the Official Secrets Act, with the accused charged with selling official secrets directly useful to the enemy and prejudicial to the interests of the state.'

The 'renegade' MoD cipher clerk, described as an 'exceptionally gifted code-cracker', is accused of leaking military secrets to an 'enemy' foreign embassy in London, offering highly classified cryptographic intelligence belonging to the British Security Service in exchange for a regular income of several thousand dollars cash. The court heard he first contacted the 'enemy' embassy in December last year . . . The case resumes *in camera* next Wednesday, without representatives of the press and public, due to the sensitivity of prosecution evidence.

As I ran my bath, I mused at length on the man I had

married, and on the practically monastic seclusion of his clubland haunt, whose habitués were members solely of the governing class, the high bureaucracy so disdained by Stefan: the 'They' who rule and judge the 'We' . . .

∼

A CAT'S-PAW.

'You do not need to know my name.'

The silver-haired woman's voice was brisk and assertive.

Just moments earlier, I'd parted from Faucon in the rear lobby of his dismal office block to be greeted by the downpour I'd earlier foreseen.

I had no umbrella.

The loo on the ground-floor presented an unintended haven, yet, even before I'd removed my gloves, the unknown crazy woman had swept into the washroom and, in a flash, had turned on every tap along the row of basins.

The torrents resounding in that tiled chamber deafened me to her words.

She brought her pale, thin lips close to my ear.

'Pay attention. Your microphone is defunct under these conditions.'

Her upper lip, I noticed, was misshapen by a scar that disappeared beneath the nasal septum. Those traces of a hare-lip told of a pitiable childhood, I surmised, and of the arid solace of intense schoolgirl friendships. Her brooding in front of her mirror must have been remembered as the most depressing moments in her life. Her appearance recalled the principal of my old secretarial college . . . whiskery, maiden-auntish, excessively severe yet, for all that, protective of her charges.

'Yes,' continued Miss Harelip. 'It's quite as you thought.'

It was as though she had read my mind, but she was referring to my eavesdropping handbag, which I'd emptied to find a hairclip.

'Your suspicions were correct,' this grim woman went on forcibly, ignoring my attempts to speak. 'Of this you may be sure, there is, indeed, in the shadows, a local surveillance team tracking you at every turn.'

'Who? Tell me!' I managed to demand, catching my breath on the brink of panic.

'*Counterintelligence*, you silly goose. Our own government in Whitehall is somewhat disenchanted with the antics of your Stefan Mikhailovich Kazimirov, particularly his propensity for taking kickbacks indiscriminately from a number of foreign powers not friendly to our interests, in return for the *notional* consignment of a vital mineral resource that he has, at present, promised to us under *similar* questionable terms.'

Foolishly, on learning this, my only emotion was one of relief that my husband had not, after all, set the hounds on me.

'From now on, *you* are working for us.'

Teacherly, she prodded my arm as though I were an errant child.

I put my hands over my ears to shut out that harsh, remorseless voice. I suddenly felt my eyes fill with tears.

'For his duplicities Kazimirov is to be paid back in his own coin. We have plans for you, my girl, and your failure to comply, I regret to say, will result in certain careless indiscretions reaching the ears of your husband.'

The dainty little handkerchief I'd shredded in Faucon's office could not contain my tears.

'You mean . . . you want me to . . . ?'

'*Spy?* To be an informant? *Of course!* You must regard me as your handler. There'll be no window-dressing. I shall call you Constance. Who needs a *nom de guerre* when a spy's best cover is her own birth certificate?'

~

I blundered out into the rain consumed by the bleak knowledge that I was now the cat's-paw of our intelligence services, conscripted as a servant of the state, a government stooge no different from my husband, the son of a judge, and a favoured nominee for the judiciary.

Miss Harelip had shown me quite clearly that the consultation in Faucon's office had been a charade.

'Be warned!' she told me before she departed. 'Every word of your conversation with Faucon has been covertly recorded, too, by our security people. The transcripts are docketed in your case file and could at any time be used as evidence against you. Kazimirov is not the only operative adept in hostile audio surveillance.'

She smiled frostily from beneath arched, ill-pencilled, eyebrows.

'Your task is merely to observe. If nothing happens then report nothing. But should you observe any act of conspiracy to suborn members of our own side then you must leave nothing unsaid. I have no power over your feelings with regard to this man – you understand that?'

'Perfectly,' I shot back. 'Neither do I.'

She shook her head in remonstrance, eyes unsmiling and lips hard pressed.

'That's as well. Dropping his acquaintance would looks suspicious, so we actively encourage the continuance of – er – your extracurricular irregularities.'

'And just how am I expected to reach you?'

'We have established procedures. You'll *know* when you've been contacted.'

What I *knew* was that I was *lost*. Lost and fatally compromised.

'I'm between hammer and anvil,' I thought. *'Damned if I do, damned if I don't.'*

⁓

Time was speeding. I knew I had waded so far into deeper waters that there was no way back to the shallows.

'There are many things of which I had hoped you would remain ignorant,' Stefan pronounced gravely, after listening to the miniature audio-tape and reading Faucon's sanitized report. 'I regret this is no longer the case.'

Faucon's 'confidential' statement recorded a week's sightings of Stefan's clandestine trysts, yet Miss Harelip's intelligence department had expunged any reference that could possibly suggest a divorce solicitor's enquiry agent or, indeed, a team of government operatives on our tail.

'Reluctant though I am to assign this new task to you,' Stefan continued in a harsher tone, 'now we are known to be on no one's watch-list, I am compelled after all to bow to my ambassador's bidding.'

He then named the particularities of the demand. In that instant I felt the pain of my heart shrinking. I whimpered and drew away from his touch.

I had dressed myself rather carefully for this hour of reckoning and, now I saw the futility of any hopes of a reprieve, I was ashamed.

'I'm sorry,' he added slowly, with averted eyes, 'there is nothing I can do.'

'What if I refuse?'

Stefan closed Faucon's report and twisted the spine of it reflectively between forefinger and thumb.

'Then make no mistake my masters will force you to obedience.'

~

YOU HAVE MUCH TO HIDE.

'What *exactly* am I expected to do?' I'd asked in despair, after we'd returned from our Thursday afternoon rendezvous at which Stefan had profitably fleeced a Latin American trade delegation.

'Oh, not very much.' Stefan had shrugged.

As it turned out, 'not very much' was his proposal that I should pilfer from my husband's study the prosecution's witness statements intended for the *in camera* spy trial scheduled to resume the following week.

'I know nothing of that side of his life,' I protested in abject misery. I had a violent headache.

'Then I shall teach you.'

And such was my distress, the headache still consumed me with nausea when, two hours later, I stood at the door of Simon's book-lined den where my husband dozed over his single malt whisky and government briefs. I recognised the thick stationery bound up with white tapes.

Papers from several cardboard wallets were spread over the desk in confusion.

In appearance Simon is somewhat epicene. Even without his barrister's wig he bears a remarkable resemblance to Dame Edith Sitwell. His is a cadaverous bloodless face. The blood appears to have drained wholly to his thin unsmiling lips.

There could be no comparison between the two men, I thought. Their voices! The deep-throated-plum-brandy-five-o'clock-shadow of a voice that was Stefan's. And Simon's spoilt head-voice indulged by Nursie; a bread-and-milk voice nourished by countless nursery teas.

A handbook, the *London Diplomatic List*, lay closed at Simon's elbow.

('When you turn the pages of a book,' Stefan had instructed me, 'it invariably falls open at the place where the text was last consulted.')

The pages which fell open convinced me I was about to faint.

Stefan's embassy! Underlined by Simon were the names of senior staff at the trade mission. Against Stefan's name was a question mark.

A rustle behind me announced Nannie Wicklow's approach and I guiltily replaced the directory. Simon stirred.

'Gracious heaven!' she hissed. 'Why in the name o' Patience did ye wake the worthy gintleman when he takes a glass? Am I not at his sairvice entirely?'

Hearing Nannie's words, Simon's eyelids drooped and he continued to breathe regularly like the blissful slumber of a contented child.

Nannie shook her head in silent rancour. For Nannie, nothing surpasses the satisfaction derived from pietistic chidings.

'Jist as well.' Her eyes flashed. 'Awake, yere man wull mak it unconvainient for ye. Let the maister sleep it off and like enough there's no occasion for the maistress to confess her offinces. That's all I wull say.'

'I don't want you to say anything – only to hold your tongue,' I muttered.

'Don't be after talkin' that a way,' she snapped.

Sometimes I felt Simon regarded me as the embodiment of an aproned housewife whose only cause was to shimmer in the haze of his faithful retainer's Mansion House polish, unfit to outrival her lasting shine.

~

Next day, in Bond Street, I had just walked into Fenwicks and approached their cosmetics counter when a harsh voice said at my shoulder:

'A concealer for dark circles under the eyes? You have much to hide. *No!* Don't look round.'

Miss Harelip's feigned interest in a sky blue eyebrow pencil was completely at odds with the appearance of one who practises self-effacement as a living.

I felt a package thrust into my coat pocket.

'Chicken feed. But it'll satisfy Kazimirov's low greed.' Then she was gone.

~

The 'brush pass', as I later learned this technique is known, had conveyed to me a number of pre-trial Old Bailey briefings, forged on bona fide counsel foolscap, of a fragmentary and inconsequential significance, constituting no breaches of national security, yet which nevertheless would be perceived by their intended recipient as 'exposing' the very limited extent of the Department's intelligence-gathering applied to the London embassy spy ring.

Such credible misdirection, I was told, would embolden the enemy to a relaxation of vigilance.

It was the thirty-first day of the month when I saw Stefan for the last time, a fact which seemed to lend to the situation a practical finality.

'Kostyusha, I have positive orders to leave,' he told me in a husky whisper. '*Tomorrow.* There is to be an exchange of diplomats. *Persona non grata.* Allegations of *spying*. The same number of diplomats from your British embassy in the East as from *our* People's embassy in the West!'

His voice was low and uneven.

'They say it's a trade-off but the penalty I am forced to pay is too great.'

My heart sang at his news: *'For this relief much thanks.'*

Though the puzzle of it all is that the joy I recognised at my deliverance was not untinged with regrets. For I knew I would never forget South Audley Street and those late afternoons of pleasure.

(Or in Nannie's venomous tongue: *'A hoor, if ye please. I've conjectured it, many a day!'*)

'There is every hope we shall meet again,' Stefan professed with a subtle inflection which simulated good faith.

I would have liked to have said, *'Nel'zya.* Impossible.'

Instead, I yielded, *'You know I shall never pretend to deny you.'*

∾

My relief was short-lived. After bruising hours of debriefing with my case officer, Faucon, in the presence of Miss Harelip, I learned that, at the Department's insistence, my cover story was to be kept intact. At a price.

It soon became apparent that they intended to groom me for another 'honey trap', in the terms of the intelligence tradecraft they upheld.

The perfect cover. Constance Bryde, the inconstant wife.

That first strange interview with Faucon had lost its sharpness. Now he seemed as dull and worn as any second-rank office functionary.

'There is no thaw in the Cold War,' he intoned, 'the doomsday clock is now set at less than seven minutes to midnight.'

I was suddenly struck by the thought that my meeting with Faucon had been, after all, skilfully engineered; was no accident. Had I broken one link in the so-called causal chain, the 'accident' of my encounter with Stefan would not have occurred.

My head swam. *Verity!* Verity had veered far from the truth.

I had no doubt that *she* was the Department's 'talent spotter', a deep-cover operative who had observed at first hand my vulnerability and, in consequence, identified a ready victim, cut out for recruitment as a potential spy.

The perfect spy. A judge's wife pledged under state oath to blend the irregular tasks of espionage into her everyday errands and irregular lovelife.

My predicament, I've been informed, is one from which there's no bailing out; my destiny to be an official night-crawler, prowling bars, no different from Stefan.

Stefan! Master of half-truths! Stefan, whose love proved false to me.

Leaving Faucon's anonymous building, I looked up at the clear dawn sky and saw the pallid half-moon half-drowning in the blue.

∽

SUPPLEMENTARY NOTE BY MARTHE COLVAINE

The narrator of the preceding account (*In Search of the Fourth Man*) writes:

'This typescript, entitled *Inducement*, was one of five such documents bequeathed to me by "Barbara Ely", my former boss; a bequest I took possession of in the oddest circumstances.

'Shortly after Barbara's death, I received a call from her daughter, Harriet, to tell me that a particular last wish of Barbara's had been her concern to ensure a hatbox containing a selection from her extensive Hermès scarves collection should pass into my possession without delay.

'Intrigued, I made arrangements for collection of the box, in which I found a sealed envelope and, within, this characteristic note:

> Darling Marthe,
> a little keepsake of all those wonderful years of blurbanity and bluff-puffery. Why my hatbox? Maybe I kept more under my hat than was altogether healthy, a fact that I rather think you alone suspected. So, rather than take <u>ALL</u> my secrets with me to my last resting place, I thought I would not deny you a glimpse under the hat. Hence this hatbox. Look under the hat! Your instincts did not play you false.
> <u>Ultimum vale</u>, my dear. Fondest <u>ultimum vale</u>.

'My delving deeper beneath the exquisite scarves uncovered a brown cloche hat that I suspect, if the perfume were any indication, had once been her mother's. Inside the hat were folded five typescripts.

'Of these instructional "featurettes" for probationary intelligence agents, *Inducement* is, in my view, the scenario most strikingly similar to Barbara's own homelife, particularly the resemblance borne by Constance's "Simon" to the "epicene" husband of Barbara in the decades when I knew them.

'I read the other scenarios (*Diplomatic Cover, Turnaround,* etc.) with ever-increasing comprehension of a mind even more supple than I had supposed at the time, and I began to see how certain things added up. And, once I understood that *Oreville Camp,* each sheet's *Psy-Ops* file reference, was an affectionate code for Stoneburgh Military Academy, all became clear!

'That Barbara had been recruited to the Applied Behavioural Science and Psychological Operations unit of military intelligence based at Stoneburgh was surely almost inevitable, given her close friendship with Anthony Blunt: a case of divided loyalties tested to the point of sacrificial disavowal reminiscent of the purges in the Communist world. To have thence taken the recruiting sergeant's shilling and signed on as a psycho-scenarist of criminal rôle-play for lectures in state espionage seems merely a logical progression.

'The value of *Inducement* to professional spy-watchers may be gauged by the series of questions appended to each typescript, which encourage the probationer agent to think rigorously and to interrogate the set text:

MI13/HumInt/Psy-Ops/F2-Featurettes/Series1/ TargetTacEval3/OrevilleCamp/Ksector-Block8.8g

From a close reading of Target-Tactical-Evaluation Featurette 3, ref. 'Inducement', consider the following:

1: Read the passage quoted and answer the given questions. Answers should be drawn from the content of the given passage only ...

I had no doubt that she was the Department's 'talent spotter', a deep-cover operative who had observed at first hand my vulnerability and, in consequence, identified a ready victim, cut out for recruitment as a potential spy.

a.) In the context of current Psy-Ops methodologies, evaluate under the following heads, and in order of precedence, the optimum motivators to successfully convert a female informant whose cultural characteristics are

similar to the target, Constance Bryde, as
described.

i: Coercion
ii: Material greed
iii: Sexual entrapment
iv: Ideology

b.)   HumInt psychologists conclude that
the three most significant motivating factors
to compel an individual to spy are "confused
loyalties", "narcissism" and post-adolescent
"societal disaffection". Discuss one of the
following vulnerabilities to determine how
target, Constance Bryde, is rendered suscep-
tible to recruitment:

i: Extramarital infidelity
ii: Approval-seeking self-absorption
iii: Mid-life crisis of unsophisticated
adventuress

2.   What is implied by the statistic:
7 out of 12 women spies are recruited by a
spouse or boyfriend? Discuss.

'Discuss! Barbara was possibly the most celebrated *salon-
nière* in London; under her husband's roof the great and the
good gathered regularly. Who can say what part a jealous
spouse with powerful establishment friends plays in the
induction of his wife into the secret burrows of statecraft.
When I think of the predicaments of Barbara and Constance,
the agency of their recruitment may have been closer to home
than I first imagined. *Discuss!*'

MARTHE COLVAINE

Filename: **Rhona**
Classification: **Infatuation**

DARKLY, MORE IS SEEN

A little madness in the Spring
Is wholesome even for the King.

Emily Dickinson

DARKLY, MORE IS SEEN.

'It's all about *you*, isn't it?' he jeered, yet on this hateful occasion he was not far wrong.

'And everything's a *game* with you,' I shot back. 'Does *nothing* matter to you?'

'*Matter?* It's a matter,' he rammed home, 'of whether *you'll* be the one regretting all this in the morning.'

A little before noon, he'd returned sunburnt to our flat from crewing a superyacht in the Solent and at once we'd had a humdinger of a row.

'You're looking more pink than you think,' I'd merrily taunted.

'And maybe,' he'd scowled, 'you need another shrink.'

I had filched an old shirt from his wardrobe and he'd surprised me mooching by the window in shirttails and heels.

Was it a put-on, he'd demanded in fury, repulsed by my hand-me-down look. I was feeling off-colour, my hair bunched up with a rubber band.

I stared at the sad-toned effigy of a woman in the wardrobe mirror and saw what he saw. My hair was short in the wrong places and long where it should have been short. (There had been a query in my case notes. 'A late onset of trichotillomania?')

'You know Dr Grünewald says I've made a perfect recovery.'

'Yeah. That's *your* story and you're sticking to it.'

It was at this precise instant that I threw more than a tantrum.

He had moved between me and the window, which stood open. His back was towards the light, face in shadow, when he turned to confront me. So he saw clearly my deliberate removal of the eternity ring he'd given me and its glittering arc as I hurled it into the garden two stories below.

The muscles in his face worked with bitterness as if he had taken poison.

He looked me up and down.

'Not my idea of a date.'

I had never fully understood withering fire until that moment.

Then he recovered his habitual, maddening poise.

'Whatever possessed you to do that wasn't you,' he remarked with sinister mildness, 'otherwise you'd be certifiable.'

I suddenly realized why he cowed me. It was because I was cowable.

∼

'I know I love him but I'm not sure I like him,' I'd confided to my friend, Ettie Klein, shortly after I took up with him.

'Lie down with dogs and you get up with fleas,' she shrugged.

(At that time Esther was studying for her Ph.D. in clinical psychology. She has since received her doctorate *maxima cum laude*, which clearly gives credence to her views.)

Now, as I kneaded the flesh of my empty ring finger, I could only rue my clinging on.

He closed the window with just enough deliberation to point up my fragile state.

'I'll concede that every woman should marry,' he smiled (as I'd often feared to see him smile), 'if you'll admit that every man should *not*.'

'Gladly,' was my prompt reply, 'just as soon as I meet a man who keeps his word.'

I indicated the supper table laid for two I'd abandoned the previous evening when he had not shown up: the two cold steaks, still congealed on their original dish; the shapeless pieces of something that had once been our hors d'oeuvres; the wilted rose in my flute vase; the unlit candle; the brooding Nuits-Saint-Georges, uncorked, undrunk.

'What say I make a late brunch?' he coaxed brightly, giving me his little smiling stare again, completely unfazed.

'The only thing I've ever seen you make for your mealtimes,' I sniped, 'is a table reservation.'

I could no longer look him in the eye. I stared hard at his feet.

Where had he been to have that chalk dust on his shoes?

~

Now is not the time to be spared home truths.

Long, long before these cruel scenes, in those early dream days of my infatuation and of his broken marriage, he used to take me to a private drinking club in Town with a tiny dance-floor. Secluded by low, forgiving lights, that dance-floor pulses to the raw vigour of secret lovers and the French chalk flies up in clouds when they let themselves go.

'Men don't like to be cornered,' was his favourite dictum. 'Besides. *You and me*... we're like foes of dissimilar races.'

'Extremes sometimes meet,' I'd whisper, reaching for his hand.

Even *then*, at the dawn of our love affair, he was stingingly opinionated and I'd often have to smile gamely until my face hurt.

Yet, I remember so acutely the *meant-ness*, the rightness, of it all.

Our time together was so splendid and vivid and rapid ... of *quality*, like the way the finest silk is supposed to pass through a wedding ring.

'On your toes!' he'd command before we attended a soirée or a private view.

He had no patience for my hesitancies, my aahs and umms, so I'd attempt a reciprocal crispness of response or adlib until I caught up.

My status as camp-follower was understood: at literary parties I was savvy enough to be one of the cognoscenti but I was never to upstage my Sigoth (Significant Other) because my Sigoth (or Visigoth, as I have latterly termed my barbarian Other Half) simply could not countenance for long a popsie with a mind of her own.

I can recall even now the characteristic hauteur of his choicer remarks.

'Averagely first class.'

'The premise contradicts intuition.'

And his verdict on his arch-rival, a best-selling novelist whose works are even more celebrated than his own:

'A small-calibre person of limited range. Man's backsliding. I'd like to see the fellow put where he belongs.'

With my exalted Sigoth, I would attend the kinds of supper parties that tolerate the kinds of guests who end up making whoopee in spare bedrooms on the discarded coats and scarves of neurosurgeons, shipping magnates, operatic divas,

TV anchormen, and, invariably, cabinet ministers and, yes, exotic dancers. Not that I sinned in that particular direction.

Except, I once trained to be dancer but my teacher declared my long bones would never gain the regulation length.

I'm told I still walk high in the instep. My waist is trim.

The hourglass figure, it seems to me, is suggestive too of our biological clock. And it's no different from the hourglass, because for every lifetime there's a last grain of sand.

'I'm no marriage-broker,' Ettie protested when in desperation I sought her wise counsels. 'Being married wouldn't change anything between you.'

'What can't be cured,' I quibbled, 'must be endured, d'you mean?'

'Foolish girl,' Ettie soothed, 'being engaged is a lot better. '

～

If you love too well, I was to find out, you're not adored.

Once, devotedly, I baked him a birthday cake. A seed cake.

'Caraway seeds always remind me of toenail clippings,' he pronounced crossly, then launched into a digression on Flaubert's *Salammbô*, one of the goriest, most lurid books of torture since de Sade, a significant tangentiality that should have prepared me for the torments to come.

'At the siege of Carthage, the barbarians pulled out the toenails of the slaughtered,' he quoted with relish, 'to sew into breastplates. *Très sauvage!*

'On the other hand,' he amended with mock gravity, 'anyone with pretensions to being *les civilisés* must speak French, at least part of the year.'

He then, to my astonishment, proposed he should accept a cultural exchange fellowship to study for six months in Paris.

That's how we came to occupy a small walk-up studio apartment behind the Boulevard St-Germain.

You probably saw in one of the glossies that absurd photo-essay on the Sigoth during his Parisian sojourn. There we are, dwarfed by a roofscape of chimneys, he, rumpled in horn-rims, *l'intellectuel engagé*, head outthrust from our dinette's tiny window, while I gaze down adoringly from an upper casement, a Rapunzel who ought to know better but is no better than she should be.

Turn the page, and there are the de rigueur café scenes on the Left Bank.

'We stay here all day,' the willing exile drawled, raising his glass, 'and drink down the sun, then we stay to drink down the moon.'

Not wholly *l'actualité* if truth be told.

On any given day you would have found me in tears.

∿

One Sunday in Paris, he woke early. The *boulangerie*, below us, opened at seven.

'I'll fetch the bread,' he offered, then spoilt the gesture by adding with a short, careless laugh, 'if *you* go the dough won't rise.'

There was something puerile in this nudge to Levitical atavism, as though my bathing rituals were some backwoods custom.

When he returned, the loaf was wrapped in an expatriate news-sheet.

He pointed to a review he'd written of an experimental theatre ensemble performing in the Tuileries Gardens.

'Any intelligent person can turn out a notice like mine,' he began with silky subtlety. 'Want to do the same? Apparently, a week in the guest-editor's chair is a condition of our so-called cultural exchange and I'm expected to sing for my supper.'

He tore off a crust from the *baguette* and chewed ravenously.

Some seconds passed before I fully understood. He had wearied of his assignment and wanted me to be a biddable 'ghost' – his stopgap junior ghost-writer – yet a ludicrously dissimilar one!

His face, it must be said, resembles one of Rodin's sculpted heads. It's hewn to that unfinished state Rodin alone could contrive. In fact, I consider it a perfect expression of the sculptor's *non finis* technique.

It is as if his head emerges from stone whose rough state is a counterpoint for burnished cheekbones and chiselled nose, coldly expressive of his platform manner, which has acquired finish, yes, but social polish only in certain features.

'Do you feel inclined to try?' my semi-barbarian asked me again. 'It's a frightful bore for a trifling half-column. You, if anyone, should be equal to it.'

Always there was some residual acidity in his remarks.

'Why not?' I managed to fire back, aware of numbing feelings of shame. 'Anything's better than *la belle indifférence*.'

When I returned from the theatre that night, I found him on the divan, dozing, his notebook fallen from his knees. Asleep, he seemed to smile *in articulo mortis*, like a saint having attained his ideal.

I glanced at the page of notes he'd last written:

'As to her prose, certain stumblings of grammar are somewhat compensated by the efflux of her enthusiasm.'

I studied again his unfinished face and compared my unfinished life of wifehood denied, all the while phrasing, as I took up my stumbling pen:

'The performance in the third act was not improved either in pairs or singly.'

But I was not thinking of that fluffed, faltering dress rehearsal an hour earlier; I was thinking of our own hidden drama of unvoiced exchanges and of how he was never on my wavelength nor I on his.

∼

I can date my paranoiac snooping into my lover's private jottings to our return from France.

One night I stole into his study and read in his diary-notes: *'Hang it. This morning again impossible to spend another hour with that woman. What can she expect when she's taken to wringing her hands all day like a Sister of Abjectness?'*

It was true. I had grown jittery and I'd begun to cry a great deal. The tears were very much like those of my childhood. Their animus would come out of nowhere. At one moment I was laughing, the next bursting into tears, strung between hope and despair.

I sensed a force-field of hostility around him. The thrilling current that had once run between us was now shorting out. I hankered for love, for affection, but found none.

Half in jest, he submitted me to a Myers Briggs Psychometric Test and, from his reading of my results, he concluded I was 'headstrong and heedless of social ostracism' of a type characterised as a 'perseverant hysteric with a Joan of Arc complex who would not be denied.'

This statement he believed to be true, though it was obviously of his own devising.

I laughed dutifully, and he was pleased to share my laughter.

'Madly contrarian,' he chided, almost tenderly. 'Admit it, my wildchild, you're open to that objection.'

It was like one of his old remarks in the days when there was no divide between us.

∽

What Big Secret, I asked Ettie one day, could she vouchsafe to me to preserve my Sigoth's favour.

'For any woman to keep a man,' Ettie replied with satiric irony, 'she must do all that pleases *him*, and endure dumbly all that displeases *her*. Are you prepared for that?'

'I'm hanging on every word,' I said lightly, thinking: *'Better that I should shove my head in a gas oven than believe that.'*

So I continued with my night terrors, beset by crying bouts that I couldn't stem, condemned to sob like a child until the well ran dry.

But was there, you may ask, an identifiable 'causalistic drive' (as Dr Grünewald might have said) to account for my excessive weeping?

In a word. Yes.

Walking one day in Walton Street, along a terrace of wide-windowed houses, I was mortified to chance upon my Sigoth hurrying down the steps from an imposing front door to which he evidently possessed the latch key.

On his arm hung a young Frenchwoman I recognised, a movie *starlette*, then bursting into bud . . . a *tenebrific* star, I should add, because at that bleak moment she turned my day to night.

Somehow, unseen, I trailed them to Charlotte Street and Bertorelli's restaurant, a preserve of loud male voices, where – as my Sigoth had once, with reluctance, explained to me – women were statutorily unwelcome and his afternoons were squandered with other firebrands at 'a sort of Hellfire Club, howling at demotic agitprop orchestrated on the People's telly.'

~

THE BREAK-OUT.

Did I contemplate then, outside Bertorelli's, in the humiliation of that selective banishment, a path to deliverance from our curdled romance?

Certainly I could not ignore the stark knowledge of my failure . . . I had to face the truth that I was no longer his handmaiden and muse . . . in recent months he had chosen rarely to touch me, even to take my arm.

He had made me an Untouchable. I knew I lacked a certain tonishness but he seized any opportunity *not* to be alone with me.

At the very end, our lovemaking had been like fighting in the dark, myself unsure of the enemy, with no weapons of defence but my blunted shoulderblades buried in the pillows, while his shadow threatened above me, the shape of an amorant cormorant, and our pleasure the bittersweet spasm of deferred remorse.

'Love. Like forcing open an oyster,' the cormorant had noted in his diary. *'I've put her in cold storage pro tem.'*

His rejection made me feel like a frozen monster, yet my first impulse to make a run for it was overruled, for I had no mother to run off to.

No. The only way to break-out, over the wire to freedom, I concluded, would be a secret Escape Committee with a quorum of one . . . a ploy which, nonetheless, raised the very tricky question of my *Escape Fund*.

If there were any justice, I thought, no defunct courtesan (and unpaid ghost-writer and helpmeet) should have to submit herself to the necessity of entreating her protector to draw a cheque.

Yet my 'gentleman friend' (as I termed my Sigoth, under 'marital status', on the last national Census) was notoriously closefisted. To separate him from so much as a farthing would remain the supreme challenge, even though this magnifico of metafiction was (and still is) filthy with the stuff.

'Does he want to pauperise me?' he complained when Dr Grünewald presented the final balance of his consultancy fees.

On so many hurtful occasions he had dropped hints like bricks:

'I swear I'll never be one of those ex-husbands who correspond by cheque.'

~

Soon I had my escape route mapped out in the same meticulous detail with which my Sigoth would pack his emergency grab-bag for a transatlantic yacht race in the event of sinking.

An abandon-ship-bag!

Let me affirm here and now, in the strongest terms, that, for a moonlight flit, *'Every Housewife Should Have One!'*

Hereunder, then, allow me to itemise the contents of an essential panic-bag all survivalists should pack in readiness for the old heaveho.

Your grab-bag should contain: Nightdress, Toothbrush, Underwear, Passport, Identity Card, Credit Card, Prescribed Medication, Basic Toiletries, Facial Tissues (Mansize), and Foldable Raincoat and Galoshes.

Forget your house-keys and address book; you won't be needing them again. Similarly, for the completest disappearing act, of course, you will not need a distress call nor rescue flares for your life-raft.

~

'Tastes differ,' was always my Significant Other's sweeping answer. 'You must take me as you find me.'

It was a demand that, at first, I readily granted. So, when I imitated his authorial style for those First Night reviews, though it seemed almost impious to ape it, he could expect to receive from me no more than the parodic.

Perhaps this facility of mine rankled with him, witness this snidery:

'I've yet to hear of a mistress whose lovemaking is real,' he insinuated, 'and whose jewellery is fake.'

We were in a bar off Bond Street, the morning he bought me the eternity ring. He was drinking his usual Negroni pick-me-up, his 'Beetles' Blood' aperitif he called it, and this taste for bitterness was a defining kink to his character.

'Feeling a bit delicate this morning?' I teased, biting my lip.

He had barely looked up from his newspaper and, forehead like a cliff, he continued to turn the pages with a maddening equanimity.

I was reminded of this scene, and other torrid exchanges and hot tirades, on the morning following the renunciatory ring-throwing episode.

It was to be the morning he announced he was leaving me.

I was in the bathroom when he found me. I was performing the antiwrinkle facial exercises taught to me by my mother.

'X! O! X! O!' I was pronouncing with exaggerated articulation.

(For drawn cheekbones, so Mother said, you must profoundly repeat the letters X-O many times, before applying Pond's Vanishing Cream.)

'Oh, ex!' he smirked. 'I thought you were praying to your ex-husband in Hades.'

(My late husband, a difficult man who drank, had been a distinguished naval commander before his dishonourable discharge for a brawl.)

'You're not the girl I took you for,' the pretender to the Next-Man-in-My-Life rasped. 'I liked you better when you were insane.'

His face was so near I smelled his aftershave. I felt I was somehow hitched to a complete stranger. Even his aftershave, *Eau Sauvage*, was an unfamiliar pervasion of my senses, though it had been inseparable from his presence for all the time I'd known him.

'You are impossible,' I murmured tearfully. 'Truly impossible.'

I saw finally a face condemned by years of cynicism and conceit, a man stiff-necked and stubborn.

'Clingwrap,' he mocked, 'Clingwrap, you must learn to let go.'

(He would call me 'Clingwrap' or his 'pythoness' when he chose to be particularly unnice.)

'How *can* we live together,' I parried, 'when I'm never *clear* as to *what* it is you want?'

'Me and *you*? *You* and me staying together?' His mouth twitched, and he pronounced my name with an ironic wrenched accent. 'Well. I may tell you now I'm not exactly putting myself up for a Humane Society medal.'

His smile was as wide as a mouth organ. If he'd been a dog his tail would have been wagging.

I must have prepared for his leave-taking because I'd hidden myself behind the fancy sunglasses he'd bought me in Cannes so he would not see my tears.

(I still have the specs-case; its slogan reads: *Darkly, More is Seen.*)

'Which is worse?' he went on remorselessly. 'Ordeal by fire or ordeal by woman?'

I examined myself in the bathroom mirror. My arms, I saw, were as thin as a grasshopper's. My clothes hung off me. Mercurial tears coursed freely.

'Why, darling, this is so sudden!' I quipped senselessly, playing for time.

I put on a brave face. 'Well,' I improvised, 'I should say ... umm ... ' then I gave it up. I knew I had been slow, and knew he hated slowness.

There had been a fatal hesitancy.

His face had darkened to the shade of an exasperated raspberry.

'*Please!* Spare me your ruralities,' was his passing shot. 'Send me a postcard.' Then he slammed the door and walked out of my life forever.

∼

I could not dismiss our parting in the light, practical manner with which the French seem to deal with natural catastrophes of the heart. In France, I'm aware, no woman is expected to remain physically faithful for three years, let alone a decade.

So that morning of our break-up I once more fell victim to the manic flight of ideas that had scorched the pages of Dr Grünewald's case notes.

Had he not closed my file, the doctor would have found me again a Bedlamite, ranting day-long word-salads until I could recover my own timid voice at last.

By evening, I had cried so long I was exhausted, like an abandoned child, my inner self now raw as weeping unrendered walls.

My lover's nature had bled me and buried me, I recognised, as I studied the stale-looking woman in the mirror whose memories of unshackled palmier days he had, by a stroke, damned as rancid.

'Was there anything more female?' he had denounced me, during one of my minor depressive episodes, his voice harsher for the intensity of his revulsion. 'I simply can never forgive your sapless fawningness.'

'Nor I such a heartless brute,' I wept.

(I shouldn't admit it, but women, on balance, much prefer living with a brute than a bore. Brutified as he was, I loved the brute too much.)

'A virtuous man!' he bellowed. 'There ain't no such animal!'

These self-recriminatory thoughts pursued me down the stairs to the communal garden where, after supper, we would often take the air.

It was a close evening of a shop-soiled day when I stood at last on the patch of lawn where the drama of the recantation of my love had been played out to the end.

'*Twilight's last gleaming is an hour appropriate to this last indignity,*' I thought miserably, as I searched for the ring, in the knowledge that my lover had undoubtedly fled to the States, where a promotional book-signing tour had long been scheduled.

I searched in vain and I was on the point of leaving when a black cat came down a mossy bank of rockery some way off, then leapt up on to the stone bird bath at the end of the path.

I saw her swiftly dart her paw into the water, and drink feverishly.

Hers was a supraordinary thirst . . . the signs of Fluke Disease, if I am not mistaken, for pathic creatures such as myself, unlike robust ones, are swift to heed the distress of fellow dumb creatures.

Such was her agony she lapped the stone basin dry.

So it was the cat that led me to it.

There was the ring, with its ember-bright rubies, glistening in the trickle of water remaining in the hollowed stone.

'What a naughty boy was that,' I whispered as I replenished the basin from a watering-can, *'to try to drown poor pussy cat, who ne'er did him any harm.'*

The cat drank and slunk away into the shadows to leave only the full moon and myself awake and, it seemed to me, the rest of the world dozing.

The eidetic image of the thirsting sick cat so impressed me that as soon as I returned to my desk I quickly sketched one of my mnemograms.

To draw in one's notebook an image seen in the mind's eye, after a particularly significant adverse event, is a therapeutic act of concentrated memory that Dr Grünewald prescribes as an essential feature of his experiential treatment regimen.

When I told Ettie about the cat and the ring she considered the event to be profoundly elemental.

'It was your archetypal moment,' she assured me.

~

TIMELY INTERVENTIONS.

I think you can see where this is going. You can connect the dots.

For weeks, I kept the telephone in the dirty laundry basket but, then, in a moment of weakness, I rang him at his hotel in New York at the obscure hour of twenty past four in the morning.

I claimed to be anxious about his health but he saw through my ruse at once, perceiving that a number of anxieties on my own account had prompted my call . . . principally, my joblessness and my empty purse.

'I agree. You are in a devilish awkward predicament,' my whilom gentleman friend remarked, in that nasal drawl of his when at his most provocative, 'and you must get out of it as best you can.'

Next day, combing the classified *Situations Vacant* pages of the evening newspaper, my attention was caught by a showbiz gossip columnist's dispatch from a red-carpet movie premiere in Manhattan.

Of those celebrity-chasing paparazzi snapshots, one photo held my eye and could not be ignored.

Transfixed under the marquee, the Visigoth grinned impossibly in the flashlight while the French actress swanked on his arm in all her catwalk glory, wearing her *mannequiné* smile.

At sight of this egregious *folie à deux* I was stricken with the dry heaves.

The pathology of love when it grows cold is to be sick with inward tensions, all the while assailed by dysphoric moods that reduce one to bitter tears, shivering like a knock-kneed coward.

I raged and wept for two days together, gnawing on the past like a dog scarred with the records of old savagings.

I could think only of the ragbag of jaundiced compliments

and faint praise that had been my portion as I compared the meretricious benison his fame had bestowed on *her*.

But, despite my agitation, I could not give him up. Not then. The fact was that, even as I seethed, I sorely regretted the loss of the brio, the dash, the exciting vibrato of the wise-cracking, elliptical exchanges that she now shared with him.

'You go back to her and *I go back to us*,' was the refrain that never ceased to sicken my mind.

'*I go back to us*' (or *'ego ad nos'*) was a perseveration that the Latinist Freud himself might have puzzled over to explain the ice-maiden's 'blunted emotions' (supposedly manifested in a 'growing detachment' and 'delusional jealousy'), which her own Eureka insight had exposed, at last, as bona fide neuroses grounded in the external reality of the tabloids.

Still, what could one expect? After all, when my Significant Other lived in Provence, he once told me, his wealthy first wife gave him extra pocket money to keep a young mistress in the village, because he'd convinced her that this was the custom of the country.

For him the finite was measured by the next dalliance.

$\sim$

'Your Prince Charming's without a single ounce of feeling,' my friend Ninian had occasion to observe. 'An evil godmother must've surgically removed his frontal lobes at birth.'

His remark was prompted by his overhearing one of my Prince Charming's more acidulous put-downs:

'*See a head doctor*,' was the message recorded on my answer-phone, '*or consult one of those nancyfied, pansyfied unfortunates you call your friends.*'

Such insensitive asides had shocked Ninian, who later rebuked me for joining my lover's house party on the Riviera, accusing me of keeping company that August with 'complete and utter baskers.'

As Ninian pointed out, my lover ridiculed others but never laughed at himself, the intent being to wound and the gibes always finding their mark.

'Of himself, though, he is immoderately fond,' Ninian insisted.

'The man's a moral relativist,' Ninian added waspishly. 'He thinks that with each new iniquity his portrait in the attic grows more handsome, despite his being the shady side of thirty.'

From the very beginning I should have heeded the warnings, but I didn't want to be warned.

∼

You might think that, surely by now, in extremis, as my world fell apart, there was nothing for it but to take my medicine and leave.

For had not that tabloid epiphany opened my eyes to the possibility of a cure for my pathological doldrums?

Or, rather, since no psychiatrist ever promised a 'cure', surely certain interventions must have suggested themselves as stimuli to effect, at least, some 'mitigation' (as Dr Grünewald would have it) of the symptoms of my neurotic disorder?

Well, on the third day of my crazed seclusion, two 'interventions' arrived in short order by the first post.

My lover's bank had sent him a crisp new cheque book, and his publisher's mailshot announced a novelist's public signing planned for the following week.

The author?

Yep. Prince Charming.

∼

The costume I chose to wear for the book-signing I won't at length describe here: a drab riding-skirt and a sober, well-cut jacket of my late mother's, and a huge scarf of faded purple, fixed with a pin of hers to half conceal my face.

The salt-and-pepper wig she had worn in her last years was cunningly teased into glossy new tresses contrived to aid my other deceptions.

Trimmed drinking straws, padded with cotton wool in my nostrils, moulded a nose so smooth and broad it defied any shoehorn to snugly fit it.

It's surprising how theatrical cake makeup, blusher, and heavier eyebrows, thickened by kohl, can configure a startling new persona.

I expect you've read Margaret Atwood's dystopian novel of ideologically-enslaved women, *The Handmaid's Tale*. Its motto? *'Don't let the bastards grind you down.'*

What you may not know is that Margaret Atwood is the inventor of the *LongPen* for transatlantic book-signings, a robotic fountainpen activated by a system that comprises a video screen and digital writing-pad at one remote location and a video screen with its automated pen at another.

Over three-thousand miles away, in New York, a writer can sign with ease his latest book with the *Longpen*, confident that – in London – his penstroke is registered by sixty different levels of gestural pressure, providing for the eager fan an exact replica of his signature at two-thousand samplings per second . . . and in *real ink*.

At the bookstore, I was sixth in the queue.

The face of my Significant Other, expectantly complacent, shone out from the video screen, his expression quizzical as some bigwig introduced him.

(His left eyebrow seems to be perpetually arched in an *accent circonflexe*. He'd received an injury to the brow at school from an OTC cadet after he'd punished the boy for a minor fault during an officer training camp kit inspection. The night of the incident the boy drank a bottle of *Bluebell* brass polish and ended up as two lines in a newspaper column. Hence, each time I felt I was being lied to by my lover, I'd experience a metallic taste in my mouth as though my teeth had just closed on a counterfeit coin.)

In front of me in the queue, an over-ardent fan with a face-lift, her skin so taut that when she shut her eyes her mouth opened, exclaimed to her neighbour:

'He's a beautiful man ... '

'And a perfect brute,' I murmured.

(*'The woman's a simpleton,'* he had written in his last diary entry, the evening before his final departure, *'and even when she's simple her prose manages to be mannered. Anyhow, I hate spare prose.'*)

There was a clatter on the bookstore floor. My forearms were so deadly thin that my wristwatch had slidden off.

4.20 pm. It was my turn to deal from the bottom of the deck and I had stacked the cards against him.

I placed his new novel, opened at the title page, on the platen beneath the automatic pen.

On the screen the Talking Head met my eyes without recognition.

'The dedicatee?' His words seemed hollow and pretentious. I now recognised the gravitas of his remarks as no more than the honeycomb centre of his moral relativism.

(On the video screen, a glass of red wine winked at his elbow. I had a paranoiac vision of his lips as razor clam shells, the inner linings glistening with mother of pearl, as though painted by Arcimboldo. Dr Grünewald has warned me of the dangers of derealization and I stiffened my resolve.)

'Just write, "For Kitty",' I said, and, as the pen descended to inscribe his signature on the book, in the blink of an eye I substituted his blank cheque.

Afterwards, standing there in the cloakroom, with the signed cheque in my hand, at last I felt myself, *myself* . . . brass brightened to burnished gold.

To the payee, his ghost-writer, in a perfect similitude of his own hand, I'd written a commensurate sum, in tens of thousands, in ink distilled from the sediment of my soul.

'There can be no comebacks,' I mused. For the beauty of the scheme was that, due to my mental history, such *pseudologia fantastica* would never be believed!

I could not help remembering the parched cat.

As I remarked earlier, a kitty is the only friend a woman has when she's in a dark place.

Filename: **Anthony Deverell-Hewells**
Classification: **Deception**

NOW YOU SEE IT, NOW YOU DON'T

Candida de nigris, et de candentibus atra.
(He would make black look like white, and white look black.)
Ovid. *Metamorphoses.*

Factors to consider when camouflaging: Shape, Shine,
Surface, Shadow, Spacing, Size, Silhouette
and Sudden Movement.
Eight Essential Esses.
Deverell-Hewells's mnemonic for the Hazards of Camouflage.

NOW YOU SEE IT,
NOW YOU DON'T

In the humdrum is the beginning of murder.

There's not much to see in our little town, but what you sometimes hear if you have very sharp ears can be as thrilling as the most lurid scandal.

Yet that first warning rumble of intent is sometimes so faint it can pass by its victim unheard.

I cleared my throat not inaudibly but my wife did not look up.

There's none so deaf as one immersed in *Sporting Life*.

Besides, she was again wearing, I noticed, her regulation-issue rubber ear-plugs, a habit incurable from the days she saw unblemished service as an aircraftswoman.

I removed my fountain-pen from the breast pocket of my medical white coat and marked an *X* on the breakfast table-cloth beneath an offensively large bread crumb.

As I remarked, the beginning of murder is in the humdrum.

≈

That Monday morning I was assigned as house-physician at the clinic.

I unlocked the door to the waiting room and switched on the *DOCTOR ON DUTY* sign.

In the convalescent ward I drew the blinds, and stared blankly at our cherry trees beyond the terrace as an onshore breeze rippled upriver to strip the boughs of their immaculate petals.

'Tawdry confetti,' I thought.

Just then I did not wish to be reminded of my marriage to Ingrid as I had begun to recognise that, since breakfast, by slow degrees, a dark cloud had descended upon my consciousness, assuming a quality of sinister significance to which I was compelled to give thought.

I shivered, and at last conceded that an acute and homicidal hatred, with all the cunning of actual lunacy, now exercised an absolute mastery over my will.

An unknown power urged me to sit at the reception desk to examine the Admissions Book beneath its shaded lamp.

A wave of dizziness unsteadied me; the ward was sickly-smelling due to the resin-impregnated setting bandages we applied to mould our surgical casts.

Since my last ward rounds at the clinic, I registered dully, a number of routine cases had been admitted.

Ingrid, as Matron-in-Chief, had instituted a simple shorthand of clinical abbreviations she'd learned from her medical records department when serving as an air ambulance nurse. This typical entry for her last patient conveys the starchiness of her brevity:

> **Jemima Small** (d.o.b. 1932): g.a. [general appearance] neglected, shabby and distressed c/b [complicated by] b.e.a. [below elbow amputation]; [both ears] a.u. [*auris unitas*] grazed; hairline fracture of u.o. [undetermined origin] a.k. [above knee]; propose subcut. [subcutaneous] repair or t.k.r [total

knee replacement]; impaired o.d. [*oculus dexter*] right eye, *lacri.
mal.* [lacrimal malfunction] and fixed u.g. [upward gaze].

Ours is a ten-bed establishment, and as we were now at full
complement I decided to visit the sick quarters.

I had ceased to be vitally interested in my work. Lately, the
conviction had grown in me that these were numbered days.

Above the beds hung little signs with cautions such as
Silence, Complete Bed Rest, Not Yet Diagnosed or *Cause Unknown*.

I saw one bed had screens round it. Evidently, the patient's
family had repaired an ankle a.m.a. (against medical advice)
and Ingrid had not wanted this butchery to be credited to our
practice.

From the street there is a view through the plate glass
window into the sick bay, which at the end of the each day
glows with a nurse's night-light.

Within, a mauve and gold theatrical curtain was swagged
to half disclose the latest patient intake, whose beds Ingrid
had disposed in two rows the length of the little ward she'd
set apart for interesting cases.

In effect, seen by passers-by, Ward Four was contrived by
Ingrid into a false, flattened perspective: an angled plane, like
a bas-relief, which recalled a painted Tyrolean diorama – a
dismal Obergurgl chalet interior – that Ingrid had insisted on
bearing home as a souvenir of our honeymoon.

More and more lately, the set-up had put me in mind of
the artifices of Hollywood where, to achieve depth of field,
midgets were hired for film sets to sit in the background on
chairs of reduced scale to create a recessive effect.

However, no doubt due to the perverse angle of their beds,
not every new patient of Ingrid's had eyes that slept. In the
dimness of the ward the whites of several eyes were open to
the street.

'Dear Christ!' I breathed. 'More cripples for her job-lot sick parade!'

There were tufts of mohair, and sawdust, on the parquet, I noticed with irritation; like the debris of Ingrid's breakfast table, this general laxity had become a besetting sin.

In the past, such slovenliness would not have been tolerated; Ingrid had prided herself on the attractions of her front window display.

Once, once, long ago, the street door rang and a distinguished-looking Jewish gentleman entered and, eyes misting with tears, he'd pointed to one of our bed-ridden incurables.

'From *meiner Spielzeugfabrik!*' he exclaimed. It turned out Herr Levenstein had been the proprietor of a toy factory in Augsburg that had been bombed to scorched earth by the Allies.

He wept as he took possession of probably the last surviving specimen of his production line, which under his caresses had responded with swivelling flirtish eyes.

He paid in dollars and Ingrid fleeced him unconscionably.

He also bought a Märklin train-set and two, nigh perfect, Halbig bisque-headed dolls.

Leaving at the door, Herr Levenstein faltered and indicated our fascia:

'Fifdy-six! Chust one schmall sign,' he quavered, 'und mit mine eyes somedings gute is found!'

Hmm. That may have been the truth *then . . .* but *now?*

56 Invicta Chambers
DOLLS' HOSPITAL
Please ring once before entering

∾

The descent into Hell is easy.

Once the grotesque problem of murder began to dominate my thoughts, it haunted me like a presence, and temptation grew apace. For mad I most certainly was that morning of the abandoned breadcrumb.

An idea had gripped my mind and no steps I took could shake it off.

I entered our Limbs Room. The door was labelled *Membrorum* and from butchers' hooks hung stringing cords for jointed dolls, and arms and legs I'd replicated in crazed porcelain.

I chose two ball-jointed celluloid thighs, removed assorted muslin knee and elbow gussets of a neutral shade, then continued into my laboratory-cum-dispensary, a bolt-hole Ingrid rarely visited.

In my *sanctum sanctorum* I lived a hideous life apart.

For a long time I stared at my workbench and grappled with wild morbid thoughts; inscrutable longings, I now apprehended, must have lurked in my distracted mind for some weeks, because lately I'd become more than usually inattentive to business.

I stood there, avoiding my own mental gaze.

My instrument trays were set up in readiness; so, to lead my neuroses into fresh channels, I commenced the repair of two casualties. Thankfully, it was a task to consume me: the work of my finest stippling brush to restore the flesh-tones of a china head.

I was free from Ingrid for several hours. Her piano playing could be heard from our flat, directly above my head.

Like piddling in a tin cup.

∿

Ingrid had taught me how to count eyelashes to spot a fake.

At the end of the passage, in her surgery, there were drawers for dresses rather than dressings. Her *Dressing Station* was what she called it. Next door was the Delivery Room and our Lilliputian hospital's *armamentarium* of medical supplies.

The nursery casualties comprised a microcosm of domestic strife . . . the plastic ear chewed off by a child's pet dog, a doll's eye poked out by a vengeful kid brother, the china cheek shattered by a younger sister's spite.

My work was merely that of a tame mechanic. Around me, stacked on shelves, dismembered dolls and curly-haired bears awaited restoration.

In our world there were corrupt dealers and we were ever on our guard against skullduggery . . . some tricksters would even go so far as to blow house-dust inside the hollow casts of dolls' heads to dissimulate great age.

For stringing cords of articulated limbs to torsos I had perfected a technique that put to use a discarded pair of Spencer Wells artery forceps.

Dr. Protheroe, our local G.P., had presented them to me.

For a general practitioner he was an indiscreet fellow; in my hearing, at least.

Of our loyal customers, a wealthy elderly couple, a Mr. and Mrs. Martremont, perhaps favoured us most. When one harsh winter they died, within days of each other, Protheroe winked, and hinted to me in a withering undertone:

'Married? My eye! They were, dare I say, more than kissing cousins!'

Apparently, all along, for over seventy years, the Martremonts had been *brother* and *sister* playing 'house' but, to their great good fortune, undamned by progeny.

'Why do babies come when they are not wanted?' Mrs. Martremont once remarked wistfully to Ingrid, while selecting a vintage Kestner baby doll with a perfect bisque head and original body.

'And why don't babies come when they *are* wanted?' Ingrid responded, raising her voice for me to hear; for, like the Martremonts, we are childless (it was a grief to my wife, but for myself a secret joy).

Ingrid's manner was extraordinarily hostile, her tone so bitter that I turned away.

Roderick, a small boy of six, who that day had accompanied the Martremonts, was squatting by our prize exhibit, a Queen-Anne doll's house.

The boy was grinning delightedly, and through an upper window pointed to a dead mouse curled on a tiny chaise longue.

(I have often wondered since whether the boy was not a phantom conjured up by the Martremonts as a projection of their guilty minds.)

Nevertheless, and this is the absolute truth, the boy did leave *one* reminder of his corporeal presence: a little scribble that had occupied him while he'd waited for Mrs. Martremont to resummon him to her side.

'Who have we here?' I asked softly, kneeling to the boy's own level.

'The Doll Lady,' he whispered, not daring to direct me to where Ingrid stood stricken.

Do I need to describe my wife when an artist greater than myself has captured her essence (and even her shop-keeping apron)?

It's a living likeness! For long ago she had reached that moment in the passage of a woman's life when, as it is said, the mirror no longer returns the expected consoling reflection and, therefore, must be turned to the wall.

～

DAMAGED MERCHANDISE.

Above me, a coda was dissolving, *pianissimo*, into a series of rills, which I knew to be a particularly tricky passage of Liszt that would keep Ingrid at her score until at least her elevenses.

Then ... that music – *Ingrid's troubled outpourings* – my fingers tensed on *my paint-brush* were, as if in answer to a prayer, all of a sudden indissolubly fused together into one fiendish artistic idea – indivisible and compact!

It was a sign.

Down the end of our garden you may see an air-raid war-den's faded arrow still indicating *Shelter*. It's now my paint store, where I stow many of the special stocks we need for our odd trade: acetone, amyl acetate, bookbinders' leather, clean sawdust, cornhusks, cow-hair, flax, gesso, glue, gutta-percha, kapok, moulding plasters, palm fibres, powdered feldspar, raffia, sizing powders, straw, vulcanised rubber, white shellac ... this is only a glancing nod at my inventory.

Ingrid has not been a major loss to the musical world ... a frenetic tinkling in a fantastic tempo, with embellishments unknown to me, pursued me as I descended the steps to my semisubterranean lair.

The tunnel to the shelter was gleaming, beslimed like the inside of a snail's shell.

I was now confident of my goal and, unlocking the studded door, strode without pause to a paint cupboard wherein was hoarded a certain *Seasick Green* 'liberated' one night from naval stores during a fleet review.

Of course, these days, my knowledge of camouflage paints probably has no equal outside the armed services.

On what grounds do I make this claim?

See for yourself. There's my old uniform on its hook behind my secret studded door. That battledress jacket was once worn by a supernumerary Concealment Officer commissioned to draw enemy fire from Allied airfields by decoy and deception ... no canvas of any academic painter (a calling in which I have gained no small repute) has ever been on such a colossal scale.

You'll recognise our elite shoulder insignia. The *scops-owl* (a superbly camouflaged species, almost indistinguishable when perched against the bark of a tree).

But I will not rehearse here the history of DG-SCOPS: the Directorate-General for Secret Camouflage Operations based at Cleremont Park.

Suffice to remark, I knew perfectly well the gravity of my actions when I withdrew from the store cupboard an additional tin labelled *Duckgreen No. 17*, a shade of camouflage paint formulated for Field Drab conversions in temperate climates with verdant terrains, and whose constituents included 17 percent antimony.

Antimony! A deadly poison when taken in injudicious quantities for, as the Ancient Romans knew well enough, a poison in a small dose can be a medicine, and only in a large dose does the medicine become a poison.

After all, the bulimic Roman *banqueteurs* had learned to disgorge their feasts with the aid of antimony without baleful effects.

So why, for my own evil ends and purposes, I thought then, should I not test the efficacy of those emetic properties?

It would require no more thought than that expended on a stupid little matter like the choice between a new mouse-trap or new vermin-killer.

I was all at once aware that Ingrid's piano-playing had ceased.

I braced myself.

A great deal of trouble lay ahead.

～

Since the earliest days of our marriage, I have often detected when visiting the lavatory a distinct odour of diarrhoea.

One day, rummaging the bathroom cabinet for razor blades, I found thrust to the back of the topmost shelf a packet of extra strong Seidlitz powder.

There was no question as to its use: without doubt this purgative has remained my wife's mainstay in her interminable quest for slimming aids.

As to the source of her supply, Herr Levenstein was not the only German to visit our dolls' hospital in those early years, for any number of dealers travelled from Krautland in search of relics to resurrect the blanket-bombed bedtime companions of their childhoods: wax dolls, celluloid dolls, china dolls, plastic dolls, rag dolls, not forgetting paper dolls, while their *kleinen Jungen* yearned for tin-plate aeroplanes, railway locomotives, steam-ships and even top grade fishing lines, a commodity very high on their list of shortages.

Ingrid was a gifted barterer, as I've hinted, and in her clandestine laxatives and saline cathartics I could now see a way to seize upon evil chance and free myself from the lowest depths a man has ever sunk.

And, moreover, it was from the warped character of my wife, misshapen by her peculiar formative years, that the necessary inspiration sprang to strike me like a blow.

∾

The mouth of Ingrid (little Roderick defined it perfectly!) possesses an underbite whose pronounced impress tells of a stolid obstinacy that was born of a troubled girlhood.

Those crow's feet round the eyes, etched by discontent, are the legacy bestowed by her mother, the daughter of a life peer. For Ingrid the Ingrate was denied by a generation the title of Honourable and, although her mother was an Hon., for Ingrid the only Hon. ever won was her election to Secretary of the Old Verenans Association.

Saint Verena School? Turn right at Darjeeling. It's a little off the map in the foothills of the Himalayas, for her father, don't you know, was one of the grander Higher Ups in the Indian Civil Service.

Among the accomplishments expected of a young lady,

Ingrid can sing the national anthem in Latin and count up to ten in Hindustani.

'*Eck-dough-theen-sharr-paanch-cheh-saaht-aaht-noo-dus . . .*'

(I have always imagined that, on our Obergurgl bridal night, Ingrid steeled herself by enumerating my exertions mutely in Hindi, to the prompting of a notional metronome.)

~

There is a deep vein of snobbery in Ingrid; that's why, I believe, she reads *Sporting Life*; it's known to be the Queen's favourite paper, if I'm not mistaken.

Sometimes, in the post, a stuffed animal arrives with its nose sucked off by an unconsoled infant. Indeed, some creatures are sent packed flat, with all their stuffing missing.

But no repairs, however seamless, can replace a bruised heart.

Her mother considered her daughter merely prettyish, Ingrid confided, and in her own quick way Ingrid sought to rectify her social shortcomings.

In a shop, say, her very public declamatory manner commanded no less attention than that demanded of the ammah who had once wet-nursed her.

'How *ravishingly* sweet but the overcharging is *monstrous!*'

The sonic mountain peaks and troughs of her emphases ran jagged through our courtship.

It was at a tennis party that I first met Ingrid Verena Merivale; she was ladling from a jorum of lemon-squash, there on a lawn by Cleremont lake.

Cleremont Place had been requisitioned for the duration and Ingrid had been granted leave to visit her grandpapa, the philanthropic peer, who'd decamped to the east wing with bronchitis.

I noticed at once her Eton crop. In India, uprooted English girls thrive oddly, their limbs assume unnatural forms, like certain trees – said to grow at night – that cannot see to grow.

I can recall her now as she then was, boyish, virginized by the fashions of the day, in a little white print frock, more than prepared to believe in the persona her dressmaker had confected.

Boarding school had been 'hellish', she confided, but attempts by older girls to bully her had failed as she and her sister would ritualistically curse them in Hindustani. (Her father spoke five languages and twice as many dialects, and was an intimate friend of the King of Sikkim.)

I never thought I'd leave my bachelor quarters for the married patch, but there'd been a latrine rumour that we were moving out (the Middle East) and, besides, Ingrid was insistent her mother should live to see us wed.

The Hon. Gorgon, a valetudinarian, had for many years appeared (I learned much later) in the *Daily Telegraph* column of *Notable Invalids*.

The wedding was a hasty affair, conducted in an atmosphere thick with bogus flattery and toadyism; for, when all is said and done, Ingrid was the granddaughter of a notable cross-bencher, and Lord Jewkes of Cleremont was the sort of nabob that could still fill the columns of the popular press.

It was at the reception, afterwards, that Ingrid's younger sister, Adelena, appeared briefly before returning to school.

I confess I thought Lena unremarkable. A fourteen-year-old schoolgirl who wore orthodontic braces. At that time she was not the sort of girl to take one's eye. Apparently, she'd considered our haste to wed unseemly and reluctantly shook my hand.

After the speeches the girl suddenly stood up and, in a harsh voice that did not tremble, announced she'd composed a song to her 'golden sister', a surprise departure from the programme that induced a drum roll from the dance band. The lyric was as absurd as it was hurtful . . .

Owed to a Brother-in-Law

Adieu, Adieu, ma chère soeur d'or,
Stolen by my brother-in-law!

'She hates me,' Ingrid explained white-faced, 'she can't forgive and she can't forget. Now she hates you, too.' Then she ran from the room.

$\sim$

The bell rang for tiffin

When I returned to the flat I was unsurprised to find the kitchen empty.

At this hour Ingrid was sure to be slumped on the crapper, harrowed by a powerful dose of the squitters.

Amid the debris of the breakfast table the large crumb had not strayed from the spot where I'd first condemned it.

To judge from the remnants, Ingrid had been fannying about, garnishing the hat of her favourite boudoir doll by recurling an ostrich feather with the butter-knife.

'Did you sign those patients off?'

She stood at the door, her voice dull and unnatural; she was still wrapped in her rumpled housecoat.

'More or less.'

My own voice was hoarse and I coughed to conceal emotions that had subtly changed. I was impatient to bring my desperate indecision to an end.

'We're running out of body parts,' I went on. 'It's the same as with most merchandise. Only two sizes – too large or too small.'

My wife's eyes were slits, an appearance not unlike the vision slits of the gun emplacements the Directorate had once charged me to conceal.

'Well.' My jailor-cajoler spoke again with an audible smirk. 'Your family were in *trade*. You should know.'

(The dart had entered an existent wound. My father had been a timber importer, which in her eyes relegated us to little more than stevedores.)

I knew too well that brittle priggishness. It was Ingrid at her iciest.

Another ear-banging I did not need, yet I'd discovered there's an insidious attraction in scheming the downfall of another, so I exchanged triteness for triteness, once again marvelling at the sheer unsnubbability of my wife.

Even before we were married and she was very young, the shopgirls addressed her as 'Modom'. And this modom-like indomitability, before which most deferred, defined her more and more as she advanced into middle age.

'I think a day's stock-taking is long overdue,' I temporized.

Have you ever bothered to count how many lies people tell? For at that second I was considering how to distil antimony from a formulation any sane camoufleur would have abandoned long before his honourable discharge.

Ingrid shrugged, so I rattled some pans and prepared to boil a spag.

~

NIGHT-TIME DECEPTIONS.
'Battleship grey! Inconspicuous? Take my word for it,'

declared our camouflage unit's senior Training Officer, 'a grey that declares itself to be a battleship is almost guaranteed to be seen!'

These words returned to me when I resumed my task at my workbench.

The art of the camoufleur is no less subtle than the deceit of a copperhead snake hidden in dead leaves.

However, it's not the sort of commission that every tyro portrait painter volunteers for.

And I'd known better than to volunteer!

On the first day of our induction course, the drill sergeant barked:

'Who plays music?'

Two limp, long-haired types stepped forward, immodestly willing to share with our sarge the acuteness of their artistic sensibility.

'All right! About turn! The C.O.'s hired a piano! Shift it to his quarters on the fourth floor!'

No. I was an unwilling conscript, like many of my fellow daubers, yet in four years of secret camouflage ops there was little I did not know about selling a super-reality to the enemy under false pretences.

As an artist, I grew to appreciate the surprising effects that could be achieved when faking landscapes, often as vast as a mile-square, armed with a giant's pallette of pigmented powders, coal-tar, cow-dung, clinkers and cinders, while wielding blowtorches and even spraying sulphuric acid to scorch large tracts of grassland beyond recognition from the air.

The cunning of our painterly techniques with sludge, sump oil and slurry rivalled that of Titian: false flare paths to sham landing strips; dummy airfields; baffle-painted roofs; scrimmed netting dyed with my *Duckgreen No. 17*; and countershading to destroy optical reality and replace it with a fuzzy meaninglessness that concealed gasometers, grain silos and smokestacks.

In our night-time deceptions, the light became dark and the dark became light. Distraction by misdirection was our watchword, and enemy spotters came to believe less their own aerial maps and more our apparent ones.

On meeting Ingrid that first time, the classified nature of my experiments forbade me to even hint I inhabited this wizard's den of secret artifice but, such was the rawness of my self-esteem and such was the folly of my misplaced infatuation, I was determined to weave a mantle of invisibility that would hide us both from the guardians of public morals ... a true hide, what's more, and not a hide-and-hope.

At that legendary tennis party, aged eighteen, she had bragged, 'The curse of a family like ours – it seems *so silly* – is we're never free of the public gaze. There is *simply* no chance to slip away, darling, even for heartbeat, without the press in *full cry*, baying for our blood.'

She touched my arm with a meaning little smile.

'Much as I'd like to *vanish*, of course. But I *can't.*'

I at once protested I would prove her words false.

'A vanishing act you want? I will show you a vanishing act like you've never seen! I will show you the truest magic to make a person disappear.'

The fervency of the magician's boasts must have impressed her for she agreed to meet me the following night at the old boathouse on the other side of the lake.

'In a trice! Without a trace!' I added. 'Into thin air, I promise.'

∾

If only I could now vanish into thick darkness as wholly as we did then.

No human eye can penetrate the dark fastnesses of the human spirit where I would wish to wander.

In the boatshed, above the slipway, Ingrid peered into the gloom.

'I see no ships.'

'Trust me.' I took her hand, leapt towards the water and, without a splash, disappeared.

I heard her gasp, bewildered.

'*It's not possible,*' she whispered.

But it was.

For three months we'd been refining a special heavy-duty marine paint that a wag in stores, because of its dead matt blackboard-type properties, had labelled *Nightschool No. 9*.

By studying the adaptive camouflage of cuttlefish in starlight, together with the spectrometric theories advanced by that master painter of moonlit waters, Julius Olsson RA, and compounding our findings with the principles of M.C. Schwab's hull-camouflage-through-downlighting system modulated by rheostats (filed in U.S. Patent 2,300,067 and devised to dissipate the under-shadow cast by a battleship by night) the state of nigh invisibility had been achieved for our *Mk. 5* experimental hooded coracle into which I'd stepped.

'It's as I thought,' I called from the blackest void. 'I'm *nothing* to you.'

I gripped Ingrid's wrists and she stepped aboard to fall into my arms.

'*Tell me!*' My grip tightened. 'Has *any*one ever mattered to you?'

'*I nursed a baby monkey once,*' she murmured. 'It was *everything* to me. *Everything* I ever wished!'

My hands brushed her shoulder blades. It was as though I had touched a razor-backed mule.

Later I took her dancing at the Starlight Rooms in Stoneburgh.

In the event, my invisibility cloak and my self-denying ordinances were needless since, returning through the moonlit park by way of Cleremont Chase, to my surprise she quite voluntarily led me into a New Brutalist pillbox, now adorned with pilasters and rustic trellises, which a foppish stage designer dragooned into our unit had sweetly transformed for Lord Jewkes into a Greek temple.

In the moonlight, Ingrid's hair was greyish mauve and her bright red lipstick had turned black, the accident of a not displeasing nocturnal aesthetic.

Her war paint, like the actinic chlorophyll pigments of military camouflage, changed under certain conditions.

But her cool grey eyes were no less grey and no less watchful.

I had been of the belief that I'd trained myself aright in night-time peripheral vision to avoid the blind spot; yet, despite all my best efforts, I hadn't seen what was there to be had for the taking.

I repeat: in the night-time deceptions of a camoufleur, the light can become dark and the dark can become light . . . so even a wary seducer can be seduced by a fledgling seductress not averse, after all, to the loss of her Hon.

❀

For steaming millinery-felt for her dolls' bonnets, Ingrid had adapted an antiquated bronchitis-kettle. It had not saved Lord Jewkes but proved to be a serviceable vessel in the processes of extracting the mineral antimony from my long-stored paints, which had since hardened.

Experimental trials on the *Seasick Green* formula led me to a yield-equation for the successful isolation of the critical poison-bearing percentage of my *Duckgreen No. 17* coating, whose spectral properties simulate the reflectivity of chlorophyll to make it the ideal camouflaging medium for deceiving spotter planes photographing in infra-red with panchromatic film.

The powerful reek of hydrogen sulphide, given off by the antimony, lent to the atmosphere a satanic stench.

'What are you hatching?' Ingrid shrieked from the lobby. 'Rotten eggs?'

She refused to bring me my customary afternoon tea on a tray.

I forebore to reply and slammed the lab door to return to my scoundrelly occasions.

$\sim$

Next day I awoke to the rapping of acorns on window panes in a high wind.

When I entered the lobby, I found the gale had shredded the morning newspapers and a sodden front page was flattened on the shop window.

A tabloid headline clamoured:

'PLOT TO INHERIT':
LOVERS ACCUSED OF
'MONEY MOTIVE' IN
SUSPICIOUS DEATH

The river was swollen and a freight of confused memories seemed to bob towards me on the flood tide.

The post had brought a package containing a porcelain doll whose mouth had the mould of centuries-old nursery pudding still clinging to its lips.

Its owner, an exacting connoisseur, demanded 'a more startled look' for the set of the thing's eyes, to conform to the collective innocency of her dolls' gallery. To achieve this look would mean fitting glass eyes destined for a smaller doll so the irides were clear of the upper and lower lids.

'*Anyhow,*' the collector pointed out in her note, '*the left eye has a distinct flaw in it.*'

A vague and fleeting discomfort juddered through me.

L'affaire Adelena!

I once asked Ingrid: 'What was your sister like at school?'

(By a curious twist of fate, though separated by four years in age, the sisters had been packed off to their English boarding school in the same semester; Ingrid had, perforce, spent four years of her early teens in India, prostrated by extreme lassitude, due to contracting a parasitic fever in the Monsoon season from her beloved monkey.)

'Lena?' A stony frown. 'She was perfectly *beastly* much of the time, "squashing" the new girls. The Juniors were often picked on by the Fifth, but Lena was a lot *worse*! Positively *vile*! From the start we were both awarded *Good Posture* badges, and I think it must have gone to her head!'

Inspired by a vague malevolence, I pressed on:

'She sounds quite the titaness.'

Ingrid was gripping a hairpin between her teeth as she fixed her habitual Alice band. When at last she spoke I was reminded of a live hand grenade with the pin pulled out.

'*Wasn't she just!*'

∽

True. The left eye of Lena has a distinct flaw in it.

Feline Lena has shadowy green eyes, green like a cat's. The undaunted survivor of a hair-pulling cat-fight (for the Merivale sisters fought like Kilkenny alley-cats), Lena was distinguished by a pierced cornea, a dark slit – in a rhombus shape decidedly cat-like – due to a fierce right-hander from Ingrid, then aged ten.

By great misfortune, the older sister's hand had been grasping a pair of sewing scissors, contrived to resemble a sacred ibis, whose razor-billed jab had profaned the younger child.

Ingrid had been embroidering a little square of hemmed linen cambric, intended as a pocket-handkerchief for Lena's birthday, her name half stitched:

Adel ...

Lena, from childhood into adulthood, had preserved the scissors and the handkerchief in a leather pouch, a grim memento of Ingrid's guilt.

The pouch reminded me of the little leather reliquary Blaise Pascal sewed inside the lining of his coat in which he reposed those divine revelations vouchsafed him in the year of grace, 1654.

That pouch of Lena's is in my hand as I write, and the less than divine revelations she vouchsafed to me alone I will now confide to you.

∾

BLACKBALLED.

But so you should first know the psychology of my fatuous traits of character, idiosyncrasies *criminal* in the eyes of moralists, I hasten to the climax of those ludicrous events that occasioned my downfall.

And the site of the debacle that skewered my early promise?

A dusty banner-draped anteroom in Buck House overlooking Buckingham Palace Road and the servants' mews.

It was my first major commission, but the flunkeys had given me a south light. The chamber was palatially glacial.

On the painting's success rested my election to the R.S.C.P., the Royal Society of Court Portraitists. An honour to be elected? Hardly! When most of those jumped-up journeymen don't know their R.S. from their blurry elbows.

So here and now let me nail the rumour that I made a play for my highborn sitter, the Heiress-Nth-in-Line-to-the-Throne.

Contrary to a widespread myth, I merely asked the Heiress-Nth-in-Line-to-the-Throne to remove her pearl drop earrings.

No more than that. The two points of light troubled my eyes.

She twitched a smile and raised her décolletage another inch.

'How would you like me?' A deliberate coy innuendo. I insist those were her very words.

'You need remove no more than your earrings, ma'am, for the present.'

'For the *present*?' Her voice had a new huskiness. 'In *the past* a suitor seldom dared ask for more than a bared ankle.' The heiress twinkled. 'Poor little me.'

She prettily arched one foot; to have arched an eyebrow would've been infra dig.

(The coquetry was now palpable. Bejewelled fingers strayed to the edge of my easel and circled my wrist.)

So how was I rewarded? Correct. The Order of the Boot.

For my transgression they blackballed me *in aeternum* from the R.S.C.P.

My consolation prize? In my knapsack, bundled together with my brushes and turpentine, lay hid a magnum of vintage

Krug rosé champagne – smuggled from the cellars of Windsor Castle – a bottle destined to launch a thousand indiscretions.

$\sim$

So *that* is how I came to be slinking home in the small hours. The hands of the station clock had pointed to a quarter to one when the last train from Town deposited me at Porthaven.

As I trod the narrow cinder foot-path that runs between the railway's boundary fence and the water meadows, I contemplated my crooked shadow in a gibbous moonlight that by my reckoning measured eighty selinolumens.

At Cleremont Park the Camouflage Directorate had built a Moonlight Vision Chamber above a circular tank on a turntable, presenting a shallow sheet of water for our crypto-shaded model warships, which permitted the measurement of all kinds of marine light effects, from the diffused radiance of starlight to brightest moonlight, so we could judge our visual trickery in miniature from the vantage of an aircraft circling at any altitude.

I was still contemplating the secrets of nocturnal mimesis, unlocked by that distant peepshow, as I stealthily entered No. 56 by the trade gate.

In my lab-cum-dispensary, fearful of waking Ingrid, I closed the door and, before I switched on the light, drew the heavy drapes against the prying moon.

You don't hear the one that gets you.

Lena came up behind me, unheard.

'My sister's dullness I could overlook,' her voice was huskier than the Queen's kinswoman's, 'what I cannot forgive is her allowing herself so few cigarettes.'

'Help yourself.' I flipped open my silver case and she extracted one of my Dunhills.

I felt a fool standing there in a monkey suit; I'd assumed, wrongly, that a tuxedo was de rigueur for that first audience at the palace.

I described, with some omissions, my irrevocable banishment from court.

'Woman's a damn fool,' Lena pouted, 'if she does not give you a second chance.'

She clasped my hand as I lit her cigarette.

(From the moment she first grabbed me she had me by the heart.)

I was now dimly aware her left forearm was encased in a plaster cast. A skiing accident, I learned, at her Swiss finishing school.

The attraction a girl with a broken arm holds for a man is not in the least degree strange. My tenderness towards her vulnerability prolonged the sweet agony of that first kiss.

The small hours. A married man. A seventeen-year-old girl. Champagne.

The awful daring of a moment's surrender, which years of prudence can never retract.

That's when Lena explained Ingrid's ibis-shaped scissors. At my suggestion, we used them to cut the buttons off Lena's dress, one by one.

Her face had shown that the same idea had struck her. Lena, I was to learn, never let the darkest temptations remain unconsidered. And, as happens to a person of weak character, I desired passionately to share the dissipation of this determinedly unreluctant debutant.

Beneath her dress she was wearing a teal green slip and crisp white cotton underthings, a comparative scantiness that revealed the greater sheen of her Alpine tan.

Lena was a looker alright.

Her long eyelashes reminded me of the spine of the glossy

little black tail feathers Ingrid would snip to repair the eyelids of her nineteenth century dolls.

(Both sisters favoured matted eyelash-blacking as their own dust coloured eyelashes vanished in certain lights and, when unpainted, they took on an albino look.)

As this rarity of rarities submitted in my arms to be unfolded, supine, on my examination couch, her docility stirred thoughts on how the mechanisms actuating sleepy-eyed dolls granted a not incidental similitude. Like our blown-glass eyes from stock, whose movements are regulated by lead weights, my sister-in-law's eyelids closed with automatic compliance.

'*Are we kids or what?*' My voice was a hoarse whisper.

When I thought of the childhood of those two sisters, I could guess easily enough who was the reluctant duckling and who the regnant cygnet.

Now, a decade later, I was free to plunder a forbidden swansdown realm.

The fact that Lena was wearing Ingrid's new, navy leather slingbacks simply redoubled my relish for our transgressions.

≈

'*Never mind where we've been,*' Lena sighed, lingering over a last cigarette. '*Just worry about where we're going.*'

I lounged against my stock cupboard, speculatively comparing the two sisters as I admired the bruised unsatisfied lips of the younger titaness.

My champagne tasted of soapwort water; I was drinking from a jar Ingrid reserved for cleaning Victorian hair-ribbons.

Lena studied me, a rueful one-sided smile reflective of a remark too barbed to withhold.

'Believe me,' she teased, 'at my worst I was never *quite* so *dreadfully* bad as to *steal* another girl's belongings.' She produced the rather grubby child's handkerchief, with *Adel* painfully stitched by Ingrid upon its corner.

I yawned: 'You believe *me*, kiddo, and I'll believe *you*.'

She invited me to share the final desecration. That emblematic handkerchief from their rivalrous childhood was despoiled as she removed a smudge of lipstick from my jaw.

I glanced at my watch. The hour hand had disappeared. Twenty past four.

The death hour of least resistance.

Lena's conspiratorial grin, her honeyed limbs, the delicate cool dampness excited on her skin . . . how wretched was the comparison when I remembered Ingrid's bridal night and waking in that chalet to discover myself married to a stick of blanched rhubarb. Even Ingrid's hand cream had smelled of insect-repellent.

On that occasion, in the dusty sunlight, I drew Ingrid's attention to a floret-shaped blotch behind her right knee, like a glassblower's scar at the base of a vase. Melted sealing wax, I learned, had splattered there on tender flesh from the wilful hand of Lena, aged nine, who'd been stamping their Christmas cards to the Maharanee of Sikkim. Evidently, a reprisal raid.

'What was your sister like at school?' I now asked Lena.

'I told her she was my friend only because she had no friends of her own.'

So, finding her ne'er so vile, I not unwillingly become her lover.

Before we parted, she clung to me one last time. In the small of her exquisite back the distinctive equilateral depressions I found there resembled the three dimples of a dice I'd thrown to clinch my winning bet.

She laughed merrily when I refused to sign her plaster cast

where the names of any number of admirers were scrawled; it was so easy to imagine her besieged by society scalp-hunters.

I could not suppress a pang of jealousy as I softly closed the door to our *fornicatorium*.

∾

The next morning, in the High Street, I caught a glimpse of Lena walking briskly towards the town's Palladian bridge; I saw her fine auburn hair bounce with each loping stride.

Before she was halfway across I stopped her in her tracks and led her to the refuge of a keystone embrasure above the central span. The river was in full spate and I could hear the turbulence beneath our feet.

'Give me something of your own to keep,' I urged.

'I feel we're standing on shivering sands.' She turned her head and looked at me steadily with unguarded eyes.

She stooped and withdrew a ribbon from the trimming of her slip and placed it on the balustrade of the bridge. Then she walked on rather hurriedly to the other side.

The ribbon stirred in the breeze and appeared coiled in the form of an ampersand, as though an earnest of her desire to see our illicit conjunction continue.

∾

THE LATE HATEFULNESS.

'Bin had up for takin' a stick to his wife. There's some as reckon she asked for it, but he didn't oughta've hit her like that. Ever so sad it was.'

The publican's wife, with air of conscious virtue, explained the absence of Dixie Meakes from the barber's next door.

I toyed with the keepsake Lena had bestowed, reflecting

feverishly on that hedonistic satiety never to be enjoyed with her sister.

If, as I intended, our 'combined operations' were to be established on a more regular footing then the ready services of loyal, ex-sapper Dixie Meakes were essential.

Everyone in our little town knew Dixie beat his wife and son something rotten but, when you saw the rows of war-service ribbons sewn on his threadbare jacket, you were prepared to make allowances for a wheelchair-bound veteran's occasional drunken lapses.

So I mouched over to Dixie's basement digs at Jewkes Dwellings, a sprawling tenement thrown up by Lord Jewkes as a benefaction to reward returning wounded heroes.

I found Dixie at his bench in his workshed. The outer edge of the door had the gnaw marks of a banished dog.

He was polishing tiny sets of dolls' teeth he'd fashioned for me from dental ceramic and sorting them into an ashtray advertising Mackeson Stout.

His hollow-cheeked warrior skull could not have been more close-shaven; behind his ear was tucked a cigarette spindled no thicker than an ivory toothpick.

'Seems we're both going to the devil,' I announced at his back and he shot a sidelong glance.

The deep-set button eyes gleamed with incalculable mischief when I briefed him on his mission.

'Goin' to the divil, suh, it's all one to me.' He gave a low laugh. 'But there's still the divil to pay.'

As he counted the wad of banknotes, I explained how I'd assigned to him a hush hush scheme of misdirection and duplicity.

So, with indecent haste, we agreed the accommodation address most suited to love letters from an incendiary bombshell named Adelena Merivale should be the town barber's shop where Dixie, a former bomb disposal man, daily passed his mornings taking cash at the door, his manhood all too briefly restored by ribald jargonic banter that harked back to the barrack room railleries he'd parried in his days of glory.

~

'If my sister wakes now she'll have the skin off us both.'

Lena, naked, was drinking tea out of a doll's tea-set while with her other hand she held one of Ingrid's miniature silk parasols.

Lying there, she reminded me of nothing so much as a jointed doll with most of the limbs pulled awry; in our breathless couplings I'd very soon learned her limbs were fully jointed.

With Lena it was not lust exactly – nor love – but some sordid, exciting mistake.

Yet, lust and its commerce done, Lena I knew would soon tire of our seamy rendezvous when romance on the lam promised altogether more enlivening adventures.

'Mostly I find the countryside dismal,' she'd earlier complained. 'How do you parlez-vous a cow?'

A camoufleur may fool the enemy but he is not in the business of fooling himself . . . I knew that Lena, unblushingly enough, would never sacrifice her rights to fine hotels and splendid fripperies for a digressional, not to say amusing, fling in the provinces; I knew I would never keep Lena Merivale without a fortune to buy her affections. She was so heartlessly well-bred.

Lesser men are panic artists when it comes to decisive action, but in those early years of our affair I was certain of my path . . . my two faked Chardins and my bravura execution of a 'lost' de la Tour paid for a decade of reckless assignations.

Replicating the crackled varnish of an old master's canvas was a technique as natural to me as my antique crazing of toy-maker porcelain.

Lena was nothing if not discreet.

I'd often wondered where in all of London she had found silks befitting a nabobess. Pretty soon, to my cost, I knew.

Curiously, Lena's signature cropped jackets, cut just below the ribcage, were invariably fashioned in silk of *teal green*, while Ingrid's own signature colour, *coral*, is its diametric opposite ... a complementary 'dazzle' colour, incidentally, of almost scientific precision ... if you examine the psychology of visual perception you'll see that when thrust together they are productive of a disturbing glare.

But, then, Ingrid would always compare unfavourably with her glossy, green-eyed kid sister from the very first moment that exquisite casualty, arm in sling, was hidden from the Dolls' Admissions register ... the doll whose eyelashes I delicately painted – each counted! – the rims kohl-lined, whose eyebrows I smoothed in feathery strokes, whose lips I tinted the softest red with a hint of Antique Rose.

A single kiss had the shockwave of a lethal depth charge that could shake one with the concussive impact to make one's nose bleed.

And the relief! The relief when that doll's glassy expression would change to acquiescence and desire!

∼

During all those years of subterfuge to look in the shaving mirror was like confronting one's accomplice.

Lena! I had once loved her horribly, yet, before long, what had begun as an idle dalliance had turned into a stifling, troublesome *mésalliance*.

In my skewed perspective, I had come to regard myself as an actor sleepwalking through the performance of a creaking play, which despite its tediousness had, like *The Mousetrap*, simply continued to run and run.

So even Ingrid's insistence on our annual pilgrimage to Porthaven Head, for a fortnight cabin'd and confined in her family's beach cottage, began to assume an unprecedented appeal.

'You'll be wanting the whitebait lines, then,' I ventured, 'won't you?'

I had grown wary, and more and more I concealed my mind from her, the more desperately sullen as we drifted apart . . . any attempts at rapprochement were met with a sniff.

Her right hand rested on the banisters. I slid my own hand up the rail and rested it on hers, but she at once withdrew from it.

I heard the tiniest little catch to her breath.

'Whitebait?' She affected a little shudder of horror. 'Oh, do dry up!'

A doll's hand fashioned from feldspar porcelain could not have been colder to my touch.

Her acerbity, the vicious tone to her voice, was due less to impatience with my conciliations, I guessed, and more to the smarting memory of an earlier summer when I'd laid hand lines in the shallows to catch the inshore shoaling of those tiny edible fishlets.

I remember I'd laughed outright, not unkindly, at the superior refinement of my fastidious highborn wife in her finicky attempts to fillet each smallfry with a fishknife and fork! Whereupon she'd petulantly declined my Kaffir-pot of excellent bouillabaisse.

On that occasion, as on this, my matron-wife swore at me

in fluent Hindi, as if I were some lousy bedpan johnnie sent by the serving-maid to slop out a sick-room.

As I have demonstrated, she knew how to talk to servants.

∾

Always each morning at the beach cottage I could easily determine the mood of the household.

Ingrid's black mood was a reigning theme, if you will, against which it was understood my life was granted the most minor filigree variations.

But slowly I became aware that this forbidding theme had ceased to wholly reign, and, if I chose, my own idiosyncratic *improvisations* could decide what the theme had to offer me.

The private wealth of Ingrid had certainly granted her a social ascendancy; and, in furtherance of this, the cultivation of rich aunts was a duty the canny niece was habituated to. And she had ready answers for the rival beneficiaries she thwarted.

An aunt who'd faded into a twilight of dementia, and at last failed to identify her favourite niece during Ingrid's routine visits to the nursing home, was shaken into recognition when Ingrid one day contrived to wear a wig of pigtails, which recalled to mind the model schoolchild she had once been.

The aunt's will was satisfactorily revised wholly in Ingrid's favour, not Lena's.

Ingrid's hair was, in fact, mostly fixed in an airy dome, as though lacquered with white shellac.

I do not wish to particularise, but after marriage I was pretty soon inducted into the mysteries of my wife's artifices and devices. Ingrid would have been very red-haired had she not been a devotee of certain tinting agents I'd discovered hidden deep in her dressing table drawer.

Two weeks after such treatments, however, all that remained would be a hank of Guinness-coloured, dusky hair.

In the early years of our marriage, she had regularly browsed a little store near the Elephant and Castle that sold hair straightening lotions, sarsaparilla and lamp oil to the jolly West Indian laundresses who drudged next door.

To see her, therefore, early one morning on the quay with a new fluffy perm, and over-painted like some office bimbo was altogether surprising.

'Another aunt?' I asked sardonically.

She flushed up unbecomingly.

'I'm *flying* up to Town. Lena has had the *oddest* notion to lunch with me.' I was pierced with a look. 'She demanded so *squashingly* I simply couldn't refuse.'

Ingrid was shod in her worn-down country brogues, and clad in her Inverness cape with a hood, which I thought more than odd.

~

I shadowed my wife in the rain to Porthaven railway station.

The London express train came and went, yet crossing the footbridge was the hunched figure of my wife, intent on reaching the cinder track that wends its way north, between river and railroad, inland to our little town.

The cobbles of the forecourt glistened like wet fish-scales on the quay.

I forwent caution, and raced back over those treacherous cobblestones to where I'd parked the jeep.

The water meadows were not unjeepable, and it occurred to me I could reach Invicta Chambers, unobserved by Ingrid, before her secret assignation was kept.

∾

The day was still blustery. I started when the trade gate to No. 56 burst open.

But it was the wind that rushed in.

I was crouched on the bottom step of my semisubterranean bunker to keep a vigil, which, in the space of five minutes, was rewarded by the parting of the curtains in Ingrid's dressing room and the sight of two statuesque figures framed by the drapes.

Framed thus, they composed a picture of newly made Arcadian lovers – say painted by Poussin – the woman classically yielding to a burly shepherd's powerful, lover-like clasp.

I recognised them both!

'Bonjour Monsieur Courbet!' I hailed him under my breath.

Each summer, wild-bearded Hans-Peter Ulbermann rented the studio I'd fashioned for myself from our disused scullery, now whitewashed and fitted out with skylights and an old slow-combustion stove. The man had a not uninteresting face, its size augmented by a very large voice.

This Struwwelpeter was the last vestige of the continental buyers who had long since returned to their homelands, content the Late Hatefulness (as Lord Jewkes had once delicately alluded to the Hostilities) no longer cast its malign shadow over their *Kindergärten-Spiele*.

Shock-headed Bluto from Krautland, I'd privately dubbed him, for in our town the painter was known for his singular resemblance to Popeye's thuggish nemesis. His beard stuck out at a ridiculous angle.

Extraordinarily, my wife was now wearing her coral-coloured toque, her face laid against his broad chest, her fingertips pressed to his full lips.

My no-nonsense wife the plaything of Bluto! For some seconds it seemed as if my laughter would be beyond my control, but at last I checked it with an oath.

The clump of yellow sedums scarcely clinging to the air-raid shelter's concrete roof seemed to mock my weakening grasp on reality.

Bluto had once disparaged our sleepy little town as the *Arsch der Welt* – the arse-end of the world – and, as to its humdrumdom, I could not dissent.

Yet, in this opening up of a second front, hostilities had been resumed, a war of principle between two shell-backed adversaries as to who would remain the true jeune premier and who would play second lead.

For a long time I stared at the window and revolved my fatuous problem.

I viewed with sour amusement the prospect of some knuckleheaded skirt-chaser, twenty years my wife's junior, believing he could out-deceive *me*, the ex-camouflager and supreme adept at warfare waged under false colours.

So I vowed to throw myself with renewed vigour into the chase . . . in my sights a green-eyed babydoll in a strapless bathing suit of teal green.

Above my hiding-place I heard the sound of a stonechat . . . *'tsk-tsk!'* . . . like the whetting of a knife-blade on an altar-stone.

I was about to re-embark on another domestic programme of decoy and deception but if a warning note had been sounded it was my misfortune to pay too little heed.

Memo to Military Intel: The more stupid the officer is, the more critical is the mission he's ordered to carry out.

~

A week later, I was stab-stitching a leather harness for a

rocking horse when I chose to break the news of my latest commission, a portrait of a Mantuan nobleman to commemorate his appointment to a mayoralty. In twelve hours I would be in Verona.

The precursory tremors in Ingrid's earlier exchanges should have prepared me for the strength of her disbelief.

At once she fell back on funny outmoded taunts, regarding me with a certain speculation.

'You're a twister!' she hissed.

With my saddler's bodkin I continued to weave the air.

'Careful!' I jabbed. 'Fixed bayonet! Never argue with an inch of cold steel.'

The whirr of her sewing-machine silenced any further pleasantries.

The Doll Lady *sans Merci* was tacking a blood stripe the length of my dress trousers, her lips compressed in a pinched smile of undetermined origin.

I thought: *'And they think to deceive me, the illusionist, whose magical arts of disinformation have confused two enemy fleets and concealed entire cities from raiding-aircraft at five thousand feet!'*

∾

In Verona I hired an Italian motorcycle, a huge Moto Guzzi.

Touring with Lena on the Autostrada reminded me of the Augustan Age and the Latin hexameter dinned into me at school.

As we thundered across the Plain of Lombardy, I was reminded of . . .

Quadrupedante putrem sonitu quatit ungula campum

. . . of hoofs shaking the parched fields with a galloping fury equal in power to a hundred horses.

Once in Milan, I could not escape the unpalatable truth that the general air of wealth which pervaded Lena's existence had to be paid for.

You would have assumed she was rich from the manner in which she dressed but, at our hotel, the veritable forest of empty shoe trees inside the big wardrobe was a silent rebuke.

The feminine soul, despite Freud's professed doubts as to its composition, is manifested in my view as a brilliantly lit shop window which positively glows in its vacuous yearning for infinite merchandise, so I prescribed a shopping spree and soon she was pepped up with the elation of a new dress . . . a little dress run up by Schiaparelli, no less.

Prowling the Via Manzoni she wore the outfit that I would most have liked to see: a teal green silk bolero with matching slacks and mules.

When, after three days, I proposed our return to Mantua, Lena gave a strange little hunted glance.

She struck the pillion of our racer thrice with her fist.

'I divorce thee! I divorce thee! I divorce thee!' she shrilled.

She confessed to receiving an invitation to model beach-wear in the Balearic Islands.

'Topper Oppidan has taken a shine to me. Says he wants a new muse.'

Her mention of Topper Oppidan, an effete Old Etonian – chichi couturier to lotus-eaters – went some way towards allaying the suspicions that constricted my chest and prevented me from speaking.

Even so, I wished we had not quarrelled on that last evening. Lena may have been a calculating mistress, but she was the only woman who could measure my emotional velocity by reading the tachometer of my heart.

～

And mine, indeed, was a sinking heart when, the following month, I spied in a doll's bassinette, on the shelf behind my desk, an envelope torn open, once secured with Lena's distinctive violet wax seal.

The seal was broken! The letter, superscribed with Topper's Hanover Square address, was written on the heavy woven notepaper that Lena, despite pleading poverty, was somehow able to affect:

> Darling,
>
> I am permanently blushing with financial embarrassment but fortunately my bank manager has agreed to give me a loan, which is frightfully big of him. I confess it. Hans-Peter doesn't love me any more. It's a bit sad actually because I fell hopelessly in love with him before our little trip to Milano but on my return from <u>Our Last Hoorah</u> (!) he states that never, no not ever, will he be married to <u>anyone</u>. I was looking forward to being his wife but that will never happen now. You don't have to write back, darling – it's not actually worth a reply – this letter.
>
> I have no doubt that Didi has told you everything. After all, it was she who first spotted Hans-Peter was sweet on me!
>
> Lots of love and kisses
> Lena
>
> P.S. It makes good Karma to marry one's muse, apparently. Or so Topper says. He's a sweetie really. Expect a notice in <u>The Times</u>. The banns are to be read at St. George's.

Didi! *Didi knew!* (Didi is Lena's pet name for an older sister in Hindi.)

Suddenly, the world that was familiar to me was all arse about face.

But now, at least, it was clear to me why, in Grosvenor Street one evening the previous week, I'd glimpsed Lena in a cab and had been given the brush-off. She had evidently been crying and was attending to running repairs on her face. Yet she had turned off the reading light above the passenger seat when our eyes met.

A snub administered.

(I later learned she had moved, for the weeks the banns were read, to Brown's Hotel in Dover Street, which qualifies as the Mayfair parish of St. George's. Her pal, the King of Sikkim used to stay there in the Royal Suite.)

I replaced the letter. In the doll's bassinette slept an antique German dream-baby with a flawed eye, manufactured by Armand Marseille in 1924.

I thought of Mrs. Martremont's dream-baby; I thought of all the war-widows we had known who'd found solace in such porcelain dolls, fashioned by our erstwhile enemy with slightly smiling mouths; I thought of ex-sapper Dixie Meakes and his dead drop for the secret correspondence of lovers ... *a secret no longer.*

∽

BEWARE OF THE DOG.

Dixie's home was silent. The door-knocker was tied up with an old sock.

Ivy had started to grow over the front door. I was reminded of a hushed mouth.

This model housing scheme inspired by Lord Jewkes was a leasehold agreement for ninety-nine years, with a clause inserted, so Ingrid gloated, to allow the Jewkes estate to buy the property back at the price at which it had been built.

The parsimony of the Jewkeses was undiluted by three generations of cheese-paring, I reflected.

'According to Ingrid, this way leads to name and fame,' I con-

tinued to muse. *'Sheer chicanery, of course, but, let's face it, I, too, have been blinkered ... dodging the column all my life because I never troubled to outgrow a weakness for cushy dug-in jobs.'*

I repeated the incriminatory words like an incantation.

'That's been my error ... to settle always for a soft number ... the cushy billet of an arse-kissing *Arschlecker.'*

There was no answer to my knock.

And Dixie's workshed had an abandoned look; on his bench, a mug of cold tea with a drowned wasp.

There was no man around the place. In a certain sense, since Dixie's injury there had been none.

In his bench drawer were a number of P.o.W. memoirs, well thumbed at passages of summary beheadings and monstrous accounts of the rape and torture of women.

In other words, the predictable reading matter of an ordinary working man fixed in his time and place. Yet no letters from Lena.

~

Very bad news rarely seems incredible.

The explanation for the intercepted letter was soon forthcoming at the pub.

Dixie, a copper's nark? No! Dixie, I was told, had once more ended up in the cooler; this time he'd hit his wife and son with an entrenching tool.

To some degree I felt I was *particeps criminis*.

I cannot deny thinking, on my third pint, that Dixie's own perfected method for removing dents in celluloid dolls (an exceptionally challenging repair) would not, on this occasion, help Ma Meakes. Nor would the small, even teeth Dixie, the dental technician, made to replace those missing from our porcelain doll-heads prove to be of any avail in the travails of his son.

The rest of the tale was swiftly concluded at the barber's. Unknown to me, Ingrid regularly deposited parcels of tagged dirty washing for collection at the barber's shop, which was one of the Sanitary Steam Laundry's principal appointed agents.

It was not difficult to imagine my wife's actions when she saw in the letter rack the imprint of Lena's distinctive violet sealing wax on an envelope addressed to the brother-in-law, the debauchee. *More dirty linen.*

~

'You can stick it!' Ingrid yelled.

It was a Condition Red situation. Her first instinct had been to kick me out.

Her eyes, long accustomed to a lacrimal malfunction, were now fixed in an upward gaze and, astonishingly, they betrayed the glimmer of tears.

Her language would have made a barmaid blush.

'Brute! When I think of how we've been through thin and thin . . . ' she faltered, her voice broken and hoarse.

Her face shone. I wanted to scour it with the powdered pumice we oftentimes applied to reduce the shine on celluloid dolls. Besides, she was wearing a pair of teal green salopettes from Lena's ski-suit, which I considered a calculated violation of the memory I held dear of that pert kid sister, the plucky survivor of formidable *pistes noires*.

That the sisters freely borrowed each other's clothes I now realised was the reason why I had so woefully misread the *tableau vivant* of the Poussinian lovers.

'Liar! liar! liar!' she shrieked, shaken by an outburst of nervous laughter.

Her lips quivered as she tried to contain her fury.

'You will be sorry you ever did this.'

She was waving the incriminating letter. The complete success of the trap which she had laid for me seemed almost to overwhelm her.

I was smoking one of my Dunhills. I allowed her to think she had scored a direct hit. The bluffery of puffs of dummy smoke from bogus craters to simulate devastation is the specialism of the virtuoso camoufleur in his ruses to confuse the enemy.

'You're not fit to be trusted,' she seethed.

It was as if her voice issued through a tea-strainer.

'I fear I can't on this occasion disagree with you.'

However, to learn humility from Ingrid was a refinement I was too proud to admit would ever be mine. My hooded-eyed hauteur gives me a look of 'languid grandeur', wholly unearned, according to Earl Smithews Jr., the literary critic, and it is this manner, I understand, that most offends.

'I intend to change my will,' my wife now declared with barely suppressed excitement.

Ingrid has a strongly developed desire to be a great lady but she can never quite bring it off.

The dull gleam shining between her half-closed eyelids was now revealed to be simply a hatred of myself.

I divined she had arrived at the moment she considered most propitious to exact her revenge.

'You will no longer be the executor of my estate.'

'And you no longer mine,' I retorted nastily. 'You'd sooner think of renting slum property to cripples than make a home of our own.'

For some reason I thought of our Queen-Anne doll's house and of the dead mouse curled on the tiny chaise longue.

~

MINDGAMES OF WAR·

Our solicitor's offices are just across the hall at No. 56 Invicta Chambers.

E. Pye and Son had been the sole incumbents of the chambers until that familial incorporation was irrevocably shattered by receipt of an official telegram (*'Regret to inform you … '*), whose subject has been long interred in Bayeux war cemetery.

Entering the remaining interiors of old Pye's offices, one has a sense of fumed oak, a sense of figures in slow motion who match their steps to stately movements from Elgar.

In his great, green leather armchair, Ernest fiddled with a paper-knife, meticulously smoothing a crease in his *Financial Times*, his mannerisms observed from a photograph by a grave-looking uniformed boy.

The massive desk was wedged into a cubby hole where his clerk used to sit, so Ingrid and I had to perch on the window seat. The office was so crammed with deed boxes that even the waste-paper basket contained old documents, some on vellum with red seals sticking to them.

Old Ernest Pye, grave as a gate post, scribbled on his blotter.

'Irregular,' he murmured, 'but perfectly legal.'

Behind my glum countenance I was smiling broadly. The application of reverse psychology had been a significant feature of strategies for military camouflage conceived by Psy-Ops, whereby a seeming transparency of motive can deceive an enemy into believing a trap has been set.

In the mindgames of war, an abandoned emplacement is often

not retaken for fear it's booby-trapped. So, contrarily, an unde-
fended position can be as impregnable as a fortress, as if it were
fully armed.

And I had *not defended* my position when Ingrid had
schemed to disinherit me; in fact, I had promptly conceded
defeat, yet protested bitterly that if I were no longer to be my
wife's executor then, sister or no sister, the treachery of Lena
should *not* be rewarded with that rôle.

If I'd set myself the task to see the inscrutable designs of
Providence conform to my own base motives I could not have
better succeeded. My ignoble intentions had depended on a
collaboration I could neither command nor avouch, yet my
secret machinations had prevailed.

'Lena shall be made a discretionary trustee,' insisted Ingrid,
who, excited to defiance of her husband, had found it easy
enough to revoke the former provisions of our gross estate,
which had made the surviving spouse sole inheritor.

'If one of us dies, the surviving spouse should *not* be seen to
benefit as a direct legatee,' she pronounced loudly.

Then she whispered venomously: *'Our will shall be so drafted*
as to favour a beneficiary beyond suspicion of malign intent.'

'Strike out that codicil,' she ordered. Ernest blinked and
struck it out.

'You'll never understand,' she fretted, *'for all her beastliness,*
my sister can still be said to be my oldest friend ... while you ... '
she paused to reinsert her regulation-issue rubber ear-plugs,
'you are a cheating snake in the grass!'

She took a deep breath: *'If I should die first, Lena wouldn't*
trust you with fourpence to the shop round the corner, even though
that sum is not excessive!'

I had expected a load of guff from Ingrid, and I was not
disappointed.

She was spreading it on thick, as usual, nonetheless, I was

now satisfied that, were there to be a future case of domestic murder, with the deserving victim a wedded mate, her testamentary meddling had ensured no shadow of suspicion would ever fall on the surviving spouse.

Outside old Ernest's window the stonechat still sang on from the topmost twig of a half-rotten ash-tree.

'Tsk-tsk!'

Warning notes had been sounded but no one wanted to hear.

∽

Looking back over the years at this ticklish episode, I can now see that my wife's success as matchmaking procuress for her two-timing sister, in her abetting of that calculated seduction of Bluto Ulbermann to betray my own love affair, must have in some part consoled her for the heartache of any number of her husband's intrigues, imagined or real.

But when it came down to it, the harsh truth was this: my wife could not escape the painful admission that her kid sister had been loved unconditionally by me and she herself had not.

I had married the wrong sister, and there is an end to it.

∽

And there *is* an end to it.

Today, I found myself in Oppidan's drawing room in Hanover Square, a room remodelled decades ago by David Hicks to correct the travesties of that fool stage designer from Cleremont Park, whose earlier decor was no less vulgar than those overblown psychedelic English chintzes favoured by the Windsors for their sitting rooms in Paris.

Topper had struck a pose at the Adam mantelshelf, as I took his measure for a preparatory charcoal portrait sketch.

'How do you want me?'

(*'Garrotted. Preferably by Dixie Meakes,'* I thought.)

Good connections had meant that, after Eton, Topper had wangled a short service commission in a fashionable regiment, but here he stood, ponced up in a hussar's scarlet coatee foraged in the Portobello Road, with a mustard coloured spotted neckerchief at his throat.

'Will this do?' Topper tucked his thumbs idly into the waistband of his chequered trews. 'You can title it, *Patrician Playboy* or *A Shot Never Knowingly Fired in Anger.*'

In some particulars, certainly the high colouring, he resembled Lord Lucan, a gambling crony of his at the Clermont gaming club, where the losses of the two Etonians were known to exceed their winnings.

Topper's floridity required a foil, I considered, so I led him to his billiard room, where the expanse of green baize and the viridian glow cast by the hooded table lamps afforded a theoretically more discerning counterpoint.

After this sitting my intention was to work up my sketches for a final portrait to be finished in my studio.

Topper's bored torpor sustained this pose of flamboyant swell for less than an hour before, with a headlong eagerness, he sloped off to change, seduced by another poker school.

'Reduced to racking sobs,' I heard the joker confide to his wife in parting.

Lena detained me at the street door. Her rose-pink lips were parted, pouting in that special way of porcelain casts, with a slightly smiling mouth.

She drew back when I caught her hand. I remembered that the warmth of her earlier greeting had seemed forced.

'This is not the way it was meant to be,' I began. 'Can't we have what we had before? There can be no one else.'

'It's the stupidest thing,' she interrupted. 'Do you mean to promise that if I lie to my husband I will not find trouble with you? Don't you see? If I insist on telling the truth to *you*, then I can only expect trouble from *him*.'

This was the closest she ever came to saying she truly loved me.

'*Very lucky for old chummy, the throw of that dice,*' I thought, '*but the damnedest luck for his challenger.*'

I gazed into those shadowy green eyes, green like a cat's . . . eyes near blinded to my finer qualities by Ingrid, and, inwardly raging, I knew I had only one course of action remaining to me.

∽

UNDER FALSE COLOURS.

All artists sometimes doubt their own ability and some artists have more reason to doubt than others.

In my own case, I did not doubt my mastery of the canvas nor my complete competence to kill the subject in the room.

Ingrid sat by the studio stove, sipping tea. Above us the sky-lights darkened as feathery snow began to fall.

She had reglued a restored wig to a doll's pate and was now teasing out the curls with a rat-tail comb.

'*In love my losses now exceed my winnings,*' I reflected. '*What now?*'

I had often asked myself the same question.

I found myself, for the first time, looking with clear eyes at the portrait on my easel, a face almost livid in hue. I did not like the lurid brightness to the complexion nor the strange, sinister light to the deep blue eyes.

'*Dead! Dead! Dead!*' I muttered, for in the portrait I saw only a facial likeness of myself.

This was a paradox not dissimilar from the copyist's conun-drum (and, I put my hands up, the fakery of copied canvases is a crime known to me), which challenges the integrity of art history by showing how much truer a self-portrait can be when painted by another's hand!

It's a sort of super-dilettantism, then, when you hold your own artistic life in contempt, your sensorium an emptied cask.

My envy of the husband of my mistress was several shades greener than my *Duckgreen No. 17* antimonial camouflage paint (a paint so named, incidentally, for the cotton duck canvas tarpaulins that we used to paint for the motor pool).

My etiquette-armoured wife stirred at her worktable, rose, and opened the backstairs door that led to the kitchen.

Her careless, unwontedly homely, last words:

'I'll just go up and look at the oven to see if it's done brown.'

Recently she had revisited one of her vegetarian phases, a baked herb and chestnut pâté for Christmas, perversely shaped like a chicken. Her self-professed innate good sense I actually considered inane.

My wife's eyes, which tend to be prominent, become more protuberant during these dieting fads, with the irides clear of the upper and lower lids.

'*Something has to change,*' I groaned, '*or I'll end up heading for the nuthouse like Dixie.*'

I keep my photographs of Lena locked in a camphor-wood chest. I burned them and the box on the stove. Soon the room smelled like a censered church.

'*Words of honour have no definite meaning,*' I murmured, '*especially if one considers that by tomorrow the despicable victim is dead, to whom honour and dishonour will be all the same.*'

The expanse of glowing green baize I'd been depicting on my canvas had grown monstrously in its aspect ratio since the portrait had first composed itself at Hanover Square, so now it was clear a commensurate volume of chlorophyll pigment was required, charged with its special actinic property to change one's perceptions under certain conditions.

There is probably never a convenient moment to commit self-murder, so for years I'd had this modest scheme all teed up for Judgement Day.

An artist's tragic *occupational* accident.

According to theologians, there is no graver crime in the Statute Book, yet I can't be convinced there is any other cure for this final nausea of life.

'St. Verena, patron saint of lepers, intercede for me.'

It's the coward's weapon, poison.

There is the consoling certainty that, with my last flickering pulse, I will be leaving those two bickering sisters the unholy wrangle of *myself* as their bone of contention.

'Last bullet, last man,' I nod. *'My life has been a sham.'*

My eyelids are closing as if with lead weights.

Feet of clay are ready to saunter to meet their maker.

Not for me barbiturates in the death-fraught glass to alert my insurers.

I dip again into my pot of deadly green antimony and raise my loaded brush to my lips.

PRIVATE LEDGER

Is it because secrecy
gains females' loud applause
that none dare eat the fruit but from
the wily serpent's jaws?

William Blake

02188	anthe	Must have analysis
02189	ahtif	Telegraph complete analysis
02190	ahtli	**Anchor(s)**
02191	ahtol	Anchor(s) and chain(s)
02192	ahtro	**Anchorage**
02193	ahtur	**Anchored**
02194	ahtxu	Anchored off
02195	ahtvy	**Anchoring**

PRIVATE LEDGER

Hereabouts, and I mean in this forgotten village at the lower foothills of the Alps, a borderland seventy kilomètres from the nearest autoroute, there is a saying: *A gossip's mouth is the devil's postbag.*

So, even when *La Poste*'s on strike at the local sorting office, our neighbours think themselves none the worse without it.

Not that my husband is troubled, should the postman fail to call, just so long as he knows his wife is silent, sipping extra frozen margaritas in her PJs on the terrace, while his ancient interbranch telecopier still chunters madly in the lumber room down the hall.

Even so.

As Neville observed before he expatriated us, 'In commodities, as in any other *tricky business* (and he had glanced at me rather sharply), there's a given number of fools for a smart operator to outwit. It's simple. Each man is against his *rival* (another dark look). By stealing a march of even one hour I'll have more local intelligence for our dealings. Therefore, *I* win.'

Neville *appeared* to be speaking of the time difference here on the frontier (we're one hour earlier than Greenwich) but I turned my back somewhat hastily for I knew my husband was thinking of Freddie Lyles, and of the feelings he believed I held for his cousin, and I did not want to face again the scrutiny of those narrowed, suspicious eyes.

~

You may have heard of his London broking house where for so many years he and Freddie endured the absolute rule of their Uncle Austin, who ordained that his juniors should wear neckties until five o'clock, and considered it proper his nephews should call him 'sir' until the day's close of business.

'Our word is our bond,' was Austin's watchword, and 'The market never sleeps, neither do I' his favourite apophthegm.

But to return to his nephew.

Freddie's looks? Well, let's just say he has the smiling open manner of a certain class that is mistaken by the world for honesty. You would recognise that sleek, well-brushed swaggerer by his bespoke, tan-coloured, waisted topcoat and the mutant white streak in his glossy dark forelock.

Blemishless, debonair, nervelessly outplaying the markets, he was labelled 'Stonewall' by his enemies yet, so distinctly good looking was he then, I fervently believe that in the City he was the beau idéal of every tyro high roller.

Dishy? Yes. Very.

The 'defining moment'?

The evening of Uncle Austin's belated retirement party I had slipped into the empty board room where in one corner hung a zoom-lined mirrored cocktail cabinet, a survivor from the nineteen-twenties; my object was to effect some minor repairs with an eye pencil.

I did not hear Freddie enter until he stood at my side.

I smelled cigar smoke and a hint Vetiver cologne.

'I needed some air,' his reflection murmured throatily; he lowered his face and nuzzled my hair, then added smoothly:

'Because you took my breath away.'

There was a burst of laughter from the last of the speech-making in the trading room and the door reopened.

Uncle Austin looked in, wavered, his hand at the small of his back; he frowned and walked feebly to sink into the gilded stiff-backed chair that governed the board table.

He examined both of us at length then addressed me directly as we drew apart.

'I've seen a good deal of life in my time.' He gestured by tugging open the loose skin of his rheumy right eye with a hooked forefinger. 'My eyes are still open, Nina. The market never sleeps, neither do I. '

His head dropped forward, and he muttered, *'Bad form,'* before he fell into a snooze.

'Motion carried,' Freddie grinned and – seizing me with the same zest with which he cornered any other market commodity – he kissed me with a revelatory finesse that could not be denied.

And I learned then with a frantic suddenness how a yearning heart can be filled.

～

Next morning, I was hanging our winter clothes in the closet when, smoothing the folds, there was rustle and out of the pocket of my evening cape fell a scrap torn from an office message pad.

It was a feint-ruled slip, once reserved for drafting cables. In fact, though defunct, the old telegraphic address from 1921 had been retained by Uncle Austin for the firm's stationery:

LIEGEMAN LONDON

since, in an access of sentiment, he took the view that it continued to suggest fealty to the mother country of the Empire he'd once served.

On the slip was scrawled, in Freddie's hand:

ATDNSHINC

I smiled. I recognised a shipper's shorthand joke. *'Any Time Day or Night Sundays & Holidays Included.'*

I smiled. Yes.

It is difficult to believe than anyone with my peculiarly slender knowledge should ever have been enrolled as pupil at a secretarial college.

~

Here in the village their custom is to cage larks. The trappers are licenced to net them under the sanction and authority of the state.

I suspect my own virtual captivity, isolated on the slopes of a lost mountain in an alien hinterland, was the dying wish of Uncle Austin because how else to explain the eagerness with which Neville accepted this unsought posting. A word in Neville's ear from the meddling old man's treacherous tongue and the deed was done.

On the day of our departure, furniture packed to be shipped by Maples, Neville had attended a final briefing in that lately violated board room. Since that smoke-charged evening, the stuffiness still lingered and he and Freddie had begun to avoid each other's look.

At midday, the meeting still in session, the telephone rang. It was Freddie from a public payphone, eager to throw me a lifeline with details of a hare-brained contingency plan for transmitting secret messages over the company's business wires.

'Listen carefully.' He spoke with a fierce intensity. 'I

have no right to show it you – and you've every right to refuse.'

'*Refuse?*' I blinked back tears. 'More rather I can't tell you how *glad* I am.'

Freddie then rapidly outlined his simple cipher scheme of a fixed shift of five places, deploying the Acme five-letter cable codes for one hundred thousand common commodity phrases still used at that time for certain confidential communications between shippers.

'I feel like one of your rusty old ships in Lloyds Register,' I protested.

'Promise me one thing,' he said, 'when your position's intolerable wire me home one word, something innocent from the code tables, darling, and I'll do the rest. Promise?'

'I promise,' I heard myself saying, and he rapidly named a place for our future rendezvous before the pips went and he hung up.

~

'But he *insists*,' our housekeeper demanded. 'The dear man, our Père Célestin wishes it.'

We had inherited the formidable Mme Myrthilde Bernier from her master, a Cambridge academic, who'd leased Neville, a fellow alumnus, his summer villa while he took a sabbatical year of study in Lausanne.

Myrthilde, I would soon learn, invariably wore a wise little smile, as if she knew better, and from the very first moment she unlocked the villa's front door that melancholy woman made clear to me that hers was the stronger will against which I would fight in vain.

'Here it is simply what's done, madame. *Entre nous.*' Myrthilde stood her ground. She unfolded her arms and indicated the street where a flock of sheep was passing, docilely bound for new pastures.

'The ordinary thing. *Habituel.* Eleven o'clock mass for *all* the village while their *pot–au–feu* simmers in old Renaud's ovens.'

Clearly, the baker must attend dawn Matins with the priest's blessing, I thought, to so devoutly superintend the villagers' Sunday dinners.

Fearing to offend, I reluctantly ceded my compliance, and that night I unpacked my black secretary dress (it held forbidden memories), ran up a modest dark headscarf, and rustled up an even humbler *ragoût paysan*.

Can you imagine, then, my hot-faced shame when, at noon that Sunday, I descended Père Célestin's church steps after the service to be confronted by a blazing Renaud Leroux. As I squinted into the harsh sunlight, he shook with an anger beyond an Englishwoman's propitiation.

'Madame! Madame! *C'est une catastrophe!*'

Soon the entire village knew that, apparently, my English stoneware, like myself, was not adapted to withstand the intense heatedness generated by an enraged French baker. My dish had exploded in his larger oven and jagged shards had strafed the complete batch. More than half the village's Sunday roasts were ruined.

Myrthilde clasped her hands and inclined her head at a resigned angle, that faint little smile full of wisdom settling on her lips.

She could not conceal the sudden look of cunning that came over her small sharp face. The effort flushed the dark rosiness of her flesh.

'*Qu'importe.*' She lowered her voice and dissembled a note of consoling solicitude. '*Ce sera ma faute!* To *myself,* the *housekeeper,* shall fall the blame.'

A paragon of virtue, she sedulously twisted her rosary beads into their locket case.

'I shall bring you some cold meats and soup directly.'

I sensed the beginnings of an obligation from which, I suspected, I would never be relieved.

~

A SERPENT TONGUE.

They say that whoever gossips *to* you will gossip soon *about* you.

So I began to fear the serpent tongue of Myrthilde and her sly familiarity, which, before very long, grew to monstrous confidences that would pick over the carcasses of practically every marriage in the village.

There are certain women for whom there is absolutely nothing sacred in the whole realm of domestic affairs, and who will talk of marital intimacies on which even the worst gorgon remains silent. Myrthilde was one of these.

'Of course, this is not the doctor's *first* marriage.'

She was talking of Dr Provost with whom I had that morning registered.

Her mouth was pinched into the tight smile habitual to her; the words were weighted with horrid meaning.

'And *madame*?'

The impertinence! I chose to answer nothing rather than run the risk of bringing upon myself more questions to which I was unwilling to reply.

Following the exploding oven disaster, I had found myself lured into new levels of indebtedness whose terms of repayment were unknown.

Alphonse, Myrthilde's husband, artfully contrived to work extra hours in the garden. *Plantations essentielles défensives*, so he said, for the mistral to come.

La rémunération supplémentaire, pencilled on an itemised chitty in a childlike hand, also detailed unrequested tasks performed by their son, Dédé, a lean agile youth with cropped hair *en brosse,* whose expressionless composure seemed bereft of humour or even the promise of its merest gleam.

Dédé brought, unbidden, a cartload of logs, hurling them over the garden wall into the woodshed like stick grenades.

He caught me watching from the window and returned the same unsettling steadfast stare, the same compressed line to the set of the lips, that so vilely characterised his mother.

I'd heard his lisping speech only once.

'Patapouf!' I'd heard him mutter petulantly as he plumped up the pillows in the master bedroom on the first day of our arrival.

An hour earlier, curiosity had prompted me to restore to their rightful places the two bedside cabinets, which oddly had been turned, back to front, against the wall.

Instantly I understood why.

On the first cabinet door that I examined, painted in oils by an artist's not ungifted hand, an idealised male subject – naked – discharged a nocturnal trajectory of silvery jissum whose notional arc was received by a similarly painted male decorating the companion cabinet that occupied the other side of the bed.

'Patapouf!' Hidden by the half open door, I'd heard Dédé's nervous outburst and I'd paused to watch as, with wrenching vigour, he'd once more turned the cabinets to face the wall.

The line of Dédé's lips had loosened for a moment into a furtive, cringing smile.

∼

Our laundry room was a sort of scullery, to be found, I

learned, in the semi-basement, a dark chamber set into the hillside on which the villa perched.

Despite its sudsy atmosphere, the villa's owner, a noted bibliophile, had chosen astonishingly to store his library there during our residency.

I examined a recess, which was wholly blockaded by row upon row of precious volumes tainted with the reek of old bindings.

A rare first edition of Whitman's *Leaves of Grass* caught my eye.

I opened its cover on whose verso an *Ex Libris* bookplate had been pasted, superscribed by a distinctive running long-hand in fountainpen.

The book's former owner had evidently composed the dedication:

Dearest Coz. 'Lips so sweet and red. Where Starlight and Moonlight meet we made our Bridal Bed.' Tears more than Kisses. Bosie. La Pietra, Firenze.

If the autograph was genuinely Lord Alfred Douglas's then this exhibit, if no other observed that day, confirmed my darkening suspicions.

For the inscription at last explained, without a shadow of a doubt (it seemed to me), why Myrthilde's master had remained the only individual in her village to be spared the wretched woman's vicious gossiping tongue, for not by one tattle had the name of our absent landlord been profaned.

∾

In the laundry room the loose soap powder was heaped in a hand-blown glass jar of deformed appearance. Whichever way

I placed it, the thing would topple until I set a moist squashed fig under its bulbous base.

Its tiresome instability seemed to me some sort of symbolic projection of all the frustrations I'd encountered from the very first moments we'd entered the villa.

That night, my prescience was rewarded by a horrid dream in which Freddie lay before me on the bed, arms outstretched invitingly, yet – every time I reached for him – my hands drew back again and again to steady the toppling soap-jar.

From the first evening of our arrival, under Myrthilde's stern decree, a kidney-coloured coverlet, with a pattern of measles-like spots on it, had been turned down on the master bed.

When I woke from my dream this hideous coverlet I at once removed.

~

'Do yourself a favour, Freddie, and shove it!'

I heard Neville's raised voice, harsh from the lumber room down the hall.

'I've had it! Get knotted!' He slammed down the telephone.

'Knotted,' I repeated under my breath. *'I think our lives are altogether muddled enough without further entanglements.'*

(We were in a fix that was ineluctable, I told myself, since although I thought Neville had convinced himself he knew *something* of what there was to know, I also thought he could not bring himself to challenge me to tell him *exactly* what he suspected I was unwilling to admit he *did not* know.)

When I entered the dim little room, the telecopier had just sputtered its disdain for Freddie's latest transmission, which I guessed from my husband's expression was the source of his unrestrained annoyance.

'Fellow says another non-compliance error in a letter of credit's shown up! The second one today! Bank's refusing to honour payment on two drafts. Minor discrepancies, but Freddie swears I'm going to be hanged on a comma if I don't go down there to sort out those finicky-persnickety *Marseillais*!

I understood Neville's jitters well enough.

If the beneficiary's certificates were marred by even the smallest deviations in the text then a comma was a large enough hook on which to hang someone.

(Despite this, Austin Erwin would have been hit years earlier by vast losses on a dry bulk shipment had there *not* been a delay due to minor misspellings in the paperwork. Famously, only the acuity of Freddie's legal brain had saved the day – he'd identified the teeniest misspellings of the destination port on the consignor's certificate of origin. From the time the product had first been shipped the market price for the goods had plunged significantly from Austin's original contract price, so Freddie, his uncle's white-haired boy, had refused to waive the discrepancies and would not pay up.)

'Gottadash! It's a time-draft and we're unconditionally obliged to pay at maturity.'

He glanced uneasily at his watch and then at me.

'*A bientôt.* Midday tomorrow latest!'

His lips brushed mine and next moment, entirely distracted, he was motoring down the narrow defile that led to the Marseilles intersection.

∼

How neatly Freddie had contrived our meeting!

Half an hour later the telecopier spat out one mysterious word:

ahtif

I opened the Acme cipher file and ran my finger down the columns of codes, then shifted five places and found:

ahtxu Anchored off

	~~02188~~	anthe	Must have analysis
	02189	ahtif	Telegraph complete analysis
	02190	ahtli	**Anchor(s)**
	02191	ahtol	Anchor(s) and chain(s)
	02192	ahtro	**Anchorage**
(s)	02193	ahtur	**Anchored**
	02194	ahtxu	Anchored off
)	02195	ahtxy	**Anchoring**

My breath came sharply. The emotion of the moment almost undid me because Myrthilde chose that precise instant to enter with her broom.

'Seems to me, madame, there's thunder coming,' she observed in her hardest voice. Since those first awkwardnesses her manner had not softened.

She was watching my face intently.

I pocketed Freddie's wire.

'That may well be,' I replied with decided *brusquerie*. 'So I must not waste time. I cannot mope around here all day.'

～

'Why did you come?' I asked Freddie.

'Because I could not stay away from you.'

Silently, I condemned myself as a pushover. The light in

his eyes told me he would never set great store by so easily gaining his object, yet he'd found something in the chase that still strongly aroused a base instinct.

We were seated in the market square of the nearest major town in the neighbouring département, a place we chose as just far enough away to be free from prying eyes.

His cool hand closed over mine. I noticed that it was unburdened by his wedding ring and only a band of pale flesh remained to denote the vestige of the marriage I'd once envied.

We paused and breathed the strong resinous scent of the pines from the mountains.

Before us, the broad promenade was deserted, an avenue of trees whose shadows had shrivelled in the midday sun. The windows of the houses were shuttered against the high summer glare.

'So many little deaths in the afternoon.' Freddie regarded the empty square with a half-mocking smile. 'I'd be surprised if post-coital exhaustion in Provence weren't the primary factor for measuring its per capita productivity.'

He toyed with the room key he'd pocketed at his hotel.

'Particularly in this treacherous heatwave.'

'Les petites morts douces de l'après-midi,' I echoed softly. 'You make it sound like some odd kind of spoof ballet.'

'You could not be more wrong. It's very real, and not at all odd.'

His fingertips touched mine and we seemed to pulse with a delightful electric energy.

We exchanged a look.

Then a mocking voice was heard to say:

'Madame Airfin! *Désolé, mais . . .* in France, believe me, a private space has yet to be discovered! *N'est-ce pas, Monsieur?'*

Myrthilde looked exultant. My unfamiliar Hermès scarf and

dark glasses had added very little, after all, to the absurd masquerade.

'The devil only knows,' Freddie drawled with a dangerous suavity.

Myrthilde gave one last remembering glance at me and permitted herself another thin smile of hateful rectitude before she shrugged and passed on.

～

'So now you have seen my worst side,' I laughed.

The hotel room was shuttered and the white blur of the shirt he was buttoning was blotched by the leak from his fountain pen when his Cessna two-seater had flown into a stiff headwind over the Massif Central in high terrain.

'Neville contends he sees little else,' I added, perhaps baiting the hook too artfully.

This remark, however, Freddie took at its own worth.

'A bad eye sees no good,' he grunted.

(Since childhood, Neville had borne a mild periodic cast in his left eye whose occurrences were invariably the effect of fatigue.)

'Do you think it was wrong of me to come,' I pressed on, 'and despise me for it? Was I very wicked?' I retrieved my secretary dress from the floor.

I had never seen Freddie so fierce. His breath came sharply with a catch. His anger with himself had almost, I thought, turned to resentment.

'I've jumped through hellish hoops of flame to be with you!'

He knotted his tie and examined me more searchingly in the shadows of the looking glass.

I opened the shutters and let in the clear, fragrant air.

It occurred to me that Freddie looked upon me in his well-bred way as wholly his right, for in his company I never ceased to feel the searing gaze of his appraising eye.

Yet any praise was to be muted.

'Well, we have behaved very nicely.' He poured another Pernod as he weighed each word. 'It would be a pity to throw away another good chance when it arises, which I'm *certain* it will.'

I saw my own hunted glance in the mirror.

'I'm not cut from that particular cloth, I'm afraid.'

I thought of the turned-down mottled coverlet back at the villa. I felt I had laid the ghost of my horrid counter-wishing dream for – strictly in terms of its psycho-oneiromantic symbolism – the bulbousness on this occasion had not toppled and, though I had eaten of the forbidden fig-tree, as it were, I had seen that it was pleasant to my eyes.

Frankly, I could find no other atoning merits in my actions, and I told him so.

'I rather guessed I was rushing my fences.'

Glossily well brushed, Freddie grinned his brilliant grin with impeccable *savoir-faire*.

Apart from the errant ink blot, his clothes were faultless. He never ever looked as if he felt at a loss, for it was always necessary for his self-respect to appear of good fortune whether it was within his means or not.

∾

Myrthilde's confidence in her intimations of a storm to follow was not misplaced.

I returned to learn from Dédé that, after hammering out a deal in Marseilles, Neville had reappeared late morning and despite warnings of floods had taken off for the trout streams that race down the gorges high above the village.

His creel and landing-net were not in the hall, and his may-fly-barbs, those wispy tufts of fiendishly wrought deceit he'd tied in the spring, were missing also.

(For as long as I can remember, Neville's passion for angling has unwittingly coloured his sensibilities. Shortly after our marriage, I overheard him in his office innocently confide to Freddie, 'Nina's a good looking girl and knows the power of her womanly ways. She's good at playing men, and . . . ' he paused, and drew breath, as though he were an exhausted fish, ' . . . and she certainly played me.')

Thunder sounded, and a mistral began to blow from under strangely massing clouds that now darkened the west.

A throb of apprehension compelled me to turn to Dédé and call:

'I must find my husband before the storm sets in! Fetch your father!'

'C'est PAS mon père!' Dédé's eyes sparked with a quick flash of anger, and then with more emphasis, 'He is *NOT* my papa!'

Yet this disavowing son was not deaf to my entreaties for he urged me to follow as, agile as a goat, he scaled the stony path to where waters flowed through canyons as clear as gin.

'Alléluia!' Dédé was the first to spot him at the waterside. 'The level's rising!'

We found Neville quite alone, half-immersed, still grasping his fishing rod, with a thread of blood trailing from one trouser-leg. He was hatless, jacket soaked, his thin hair matted in the rain. He had kicked off one of his waders.

'Foot stuck fast under ledge.' He bit his lip as if stung by a bitter taste. 'You came *too soon*, Nina! Only a fool allows himself to be *so easily caught.*'

Dédé at once clambered across the rocks, ducked under the water and released him. Then the lad was at Neville like a terrier, lifting him bodily from the water, and tenderly depositing him on the bank, now the very model of a pastoral Ganymede as he pressed a flask of brandy to my husband's lips.

'Another minute and we would have lost you, *Monsieur*.'

The youth knelt beside him, in an attitude of almost filial devotion, as if an archetypal figure from his inner dramas had at last assumed its rightful place in a long awaited emotional tableau whose composition was now finally resolved.

Neville gave a short laugh, and looked keenly into my face,.

'Better I should die in my own marriage bed, you mean,' he remarked with ghastly sarcasm, 'than be drowned like a rat in a trap! Is that it?'

He raised himself on one arm, he face deathly pale, then fainted.

In the slicing wind, numbed by driven rain, we somehow retreated to the villa, stumbling through the scrub like the last remnants of a vanquished army.

∾

From the very beginning of Neville's fevered sickness I scented meddling in the village, and collusion as pungent as a fox.

'How I feel for you, madame, in your troubles!'

Myrthilde's clasped hands, expressive of respectful dutifulness, belied the taunt. 'I cannot say how sorry I am to see your husband brought so low.'

'And I am sorry you see things that do not exist,' I countered snappishly.

I bent over the bed and smoothed Neville's brow. As he slept, his hands picked fitfully at the hem of the kidney-coloured coverlet.

Myrthilde's face remained a submissive blank, yet her calculating eyes were fixed intently on me.

In guarding our secret, she took pleasure in my discomfiture, seeking in every domestic task a chance to test the extent of her new power, wishing to gratify her love of it with evidence of it in our lives.

'Dr Provost is not to be trusted,' she declared. 'We must visit the *healer*. Please follow me.' It was not a request but an order.

~

Myrthilde led me across a courtyard chequered with clumps of lavender; the tulips in the flower beds were as pink as coconut ice.

It was a fresh morning, with a keen breeze from the pass.

The poignant scent of aromatic shrubs filled the air – myrtle, cistus, tamarisk – blended with odours from a herb garden beyond a cottage wall.

The outhouse of the healer was as fresh and cool as a dairy, and a faint clean smell of sanitary fluid and wax polish rose from its tiled floor.

Involuntarily I gasped.

A heavy workbench commanded the centre of the room. On it lay a pale human torso composed of extraordinarily shaped medicinal urns, each flacon faithfully moulded in porcelain to the shape of a principal body-part: torso; breastplate; lungs; heart; trachea and oesophagus; diaphragm; stomach; liver; pancreas and spleen; bladder and uterus; and intestines.

I noted there were interchangeable sex organs.

A man cleared his throat behind me.

Renaud Leroux stood in the doorway.

'You seek a cure, madame?' The smirk was unmistakeable.

It was an unpleasant surprise to learn how much the village despised me.

'A weakness *here*, you may be sure,' Myrthilde put in, with a meaning look, placing her hand on the porcelain heart.

I had thought the French to be martyrs to *la maladie imaginaire*, and never imagined – until to my horror I read the healer's tariff – that it was perfectly commonplace for folk from the backwoods to suffer from black eyes, broken teeth, cracked ribs and swollen lips . . . no wonder, then, according to Myrthilde, so many marriages in that village had not survived the bridal bed's first raptures (including hers?).

The stone cold mannikin on the bench with its removable viscera and detachable genitalia and brain seemed more than emblematic of the primitive natives of those parts whose innards craved roasted lark, a delicacy the heartless trapper fattened in a darkened cage, drowned in Armagnac, then ate whole, bones and all, while covering his head with a large napkin to hide from the wrath of God.

I paid wily old Leroux an extortionate sum coaxed out of me by Myrthilde, and was handed a nonsensical herbal tincture, while across each face shimmered more than the ghost of a sneer.

Emerging into sunlight, I contemplated the paradisiacal symmetry of the vine leaves and oleander sprays – their regularity of growth as perfect as any Acanthus leaf on a Corinthian pillar – and considered how in such a stillness of warmth so many lives seemed misshapened by uncertain prevailing winds.

∿

DOUBLE ACCOUNTING.

I poured the herbalist's nostrum down the loo.

At length, I approached where Neville slept.

'I must send for Dr Provost,' I began very gently, and sat

close beside the bed. 'He can do so much more than … ' My voice trailed off brokenly.

Suddenly his lips moved. I knelt and laid one arm across his chest. I felt his heart give a great bound.

'Is it quite hopeless?' He opened his eyes, bright with fever.

His fingers wandered from the counterpane and searched for mine.

'That's better,' he mumbled. 'It's good to have you back.'

I noticed his strabismic left eye was more pronounced due to fatigue and, intuitively, he must have seen my looking and my quick evasive glance, because, seemingly without a non sequitur, he struggled to say more:

'Nothing has changed. How do you suppose I came by this?' Neville pointed to his left eye. 'From our earliest boyhood Freddie was jealous of what I had, and always wanted what was mine.'

Neville then haltingly explained how Freddie, aged twelve, had fought with his younger cousin on a summer beach for possession of Neville's new .22 air rifle. The gun went off and a pellet the size of a small pea lodged between his eyeball and the surrounding socket. In defence, Neville had blindly lashed out with the gun butt, dealing Freddie a savage blow to the head, the scar from which had later sprouted that trademark dark forelock, now dashed with the white blaze of a mustang.

'It was just the beginning of our school hols at Deal. After that, I was somewhat handicapped in an unfair competition. And, *even now* … ' Neville's shrewd glance was now steady on me, ' … I'm afraid I'll never quite measure up to Freddie in his Speedos.'

I took his hand and felt for his pulse.

There was a long silence.

'Don't be so sure,' I improvised, 'it is not too late.' And my husband laughed easily, and drifted into contented sleep.

~

No longer did I fear my secret being discovered by the world.

At once I sped to Dr Provost, with my contempt for false Myrthilde and her too eager tongue magnified a thousandfold.

And very soon I stood in the village doctor's consulting rooms, choked full with righteous anger, and primed to confront him with my long-held smouldering grievances.

'The woman is a malign and pernicious rumourmonger,' I reproached him. 'Why, because of her own dire marital history, this *dreadful woman* regards second marriages as an admission of failure! Even *yours,* so she has led me to believe.'

I waited with satisfaction for the thrust to drive home but, confusingly, I saw only the wrong answer in his face. I saw that I had struck a false note.

'On the contrary,' Dr Provost returned grimly, 'my first wife drowned on the first day of our honeymoon. A *first* marriage, yes. But I fear any failure there is . . . is in the *interprétation*.'

I disliked his too close a scrutiny of my face, for it was a face now suffused with abjectest shame.

~

It occurs to me, only now, that when, at Uncle Austin's leaving party, one of the brokers, a Harrovian, had called for 'Three chairs' and subdued cheers from the assembly followed, the future chairmanship of the brokerage had been hanging in the balance, and Freddie the favourite nephew had actually, even then, been playing a long game to secure it.

Neville once told me that, to outsmart the Revenue, Freddie kept two sets of books for stock audits, an 'official' set and a private 'shadow' ledger only he and Uncle Austin ever saw.

Indeed, such bending of the rules for shipping dry bulk commodities had been established by their family as far back as the old East India exchange.

'Double accounting,' Neville had concluded with something very nearly approaching contempt, still smarting (I now saw) from a grudge which he had never laid aside since boyhood. 'As in all things, Freddie wants always to be in perfect control.'

His remark was like a depth charge that had detonated only much later.

I saw it was true. However false the manoeuvre, Freddie performed it thoroughly and carefully, without the least intention of regretting it afterwards. Freddie's passion to make money, I now knew, was stronger than any that had seized him in pursuit of women.

He did 'himself well,' to repeat Neville's phrase, in a large Surrey mansion. His wife, Divinia, was a Soroptimist who taught historic floristry and the language of flowers to curators at stately homes.

In future, I reflected, were I to again dream covetously of the homelife of leggy Vinia Lyles, the emotions I'd be sure to feel would be neither sisterly nor optimistic.

Freddie once told me he knew how to stow an elephant in the hold of a freighter. It required twenty-five gallons of water a day to slake its thirst.

In my all-consuming craving for Freddie, I knew that I was held by a false elation, yet already I'd begun to regret the loss.

In all truth, I'd seen no other fate for myself since that night at the shipping office when I was so very struck with him.

Freddie would ever be the consignor and I the consignee.

It was clear to us both that we had still a long, long journey before us.

The Christmas following that *année folle*, I bought Freddie a Montblanc fountainpen, a *Traveller*, which is supplied in a special case in order that it might be stored with its nib upright, when we're flying.

It has special properties, you see, and, if it's screwed up tightly enough, it resists the pressure changes with the admirable certainty of no leaks.

NOTES AND OBSERVATIONS ON CASE HISTORIES

Theresa Ollivante (*A Room to the End of Fall.*)

In 2008, when a notice heralding this narrative first appeared (*Thought Police*, see page 414 of Catherine Eisner's *Sister Morphine* published by Salt), the announcement concluded that '. . . when, even the Press have so far failed to uncover clues to solve the mystery of her disappearance, tantalisingly, the publication of a full account of her astonishing story must be delayed until the next edition of this work [i.e. *Sister Morphine*].'

This earlier commentary observed that, frustratingly, the occasion of Theresa's *disappearance*, corroborated by a number of witnesses, had been more closely documented and reported more faithfully than the bizarre circumstances of her *discovery*.

In *Thought Police* there is a sketch of the scene outside Theresa's city apartment house, the day before her disappearance, that gave rise to the narrative's title. A police patrol car halts beside her as she stands immobile in an unseasonable flurry of snow, dressed in a thin housecoat, staring fixedly at a drain cover where the snowfall had melted in a perfect dish-shaped concavity.

The cops are friendly and polite.

They had merely put to her one question: 'Something on your mind, maybe?'

'No. It's nothing,' she answers dryly with a false smile. 'Unless, perhaps, you're a deputation from the Thought Police.'

A day later she vanishes without a trace to reemerge half a decade later.

In *Thought Police* in 2008 there are quoted a few key passages from her diary into which she had copied extracts from Chekhov's sinister cautionary tale, *The Bet,* whose unnamed young hero has himself incarcerated voluntarily for fifteen years in a well-stocked library – in solitary confinement – to win a bet of two million roubles wagered by a banker.

'The prisoner (writes Theresa), amazingly, in four years, reads over *six hundred volumes* and when, after fifteen years of confinement in which he imbibes the world's classics, he emerges into daylight, his appearance is almost spectral. His face is yellow, his cheeks are hollow, his hair is streaked with silver, and no one can believe that he is only forty! He is a skeleton with the skin drawn tight over his bones and long matted curls like . . . like, well, like my own, if I'm honest. But what does the prisoner declare upon his release that I would not myself assert were I to meet that hateful unconscionable banker!?

' "Your books have given me wisdom. All man's unresting thought from the ages is compressed into the small compass of my brain. I know that I am wiser than all of you. And I despise your books, as I despise wisdom and the blessings of this world. It is all worthless, fleeting, illusory, and deceptive, like a mirage . . . as though you were no more than mice burrowing under the floor . . ." '

Theresa evidently empathised strongly with Chekhov's disillusioned bookish captive, but she herself denied at the time a

Freudo-Marxist view of alienation to explain her own anomie and other related neurotica.

Despite admitting to severe psychological adjustment problems, she claimed her sense of dislocation from a once familiar world was due, essentially, to the extreme mistrust and suspicion with which she regarded her literary agent, Sherman Seymour Dane. Specifically, she falsely accused Dane of *ghostwriting* the major portion of her novel, *An Auroral Stain*, which was published to mixed reviews during her enforced absence. 'For Seymour, it was more than a case of *corpus delicti* when I disappeared,' Theresa alleged, 'it was a case of a missing opus whose inconvenient absence was remedied when he presumed to "complete" the work without my authorisation.'

That she was *wholly misguided* in this belief the narrative, *A Room to the End of Fall* now happily makes clear.

Lewis Carroll and Kepler von Thul (*A Bad Case*.)

The British Stammering Association cites Carroll's *The Hunting of the Snark* as offering a revealing insight into the anguish of an inveterate stammerer ('Do-do' Dodgson) who '... *with senseless grimaces endeavoured to say/What his tongue could no longer express.*'

Although the Reverend Robinson Duckworth (the model for 'the Duck' in *Alice*) was present in the original boating expedition of 4 July 1862 during which *Alice's Adventures* were first told by Lewis Carroll, the events described in von Thul's letter took place in June of the following year.

The weekend of Saturday June 27 1863 is, indeed, a remarkable date since, critically, it coincides with a page of entries missing from Lewis Carroll's diary for that period, about which there is immense and fanciful speculation by Carrollian scholars (including the supposition that on that day he proposed marriage to Alice Liddell, then 11 years old, an incautious impulse for which the Liddell family shunned him, a painful breach that took some months to heal). The page's excision, judged now by the foregoing fragments recorded by von Thul, suggests a contemporary act of self-mutilation rather than a calculated redaction by Dodgson heirs to preserve the 'dead sanctities' of their grossly mythologised forebear of illustrious memory.

Kepler von Thul, direct descendent of the German mathematician, astronomer and astrologer, Johannes Kepler, was infamous throughout Central Europe as author of *Die Fledermauskinder* (*The Bat Children*), a vampiric novel that rivals in horror *The Vampyre* by Polidori, published some three decades earlier. The manuscript leaf of Leibnitzian logical calculi in the possession of Eisner, addressed to Lewis Carroll and signed, *Kepler von Thul, Oktober 9 1863, Leipzig*, contains a mathematical derivation proving *Zero* is equal to *One*. On the same sheet, Kepler, by extension, develops an algebraic argument to prove *Good* equates with *Evil*. As Lewis Carroll's cryptic clues more than hint, the grotesque characterisation of the Mad Hatter in *Alice* should doubtless be taken to lampoon the malign logic-chopping mania of Kepler at its most extreme. (*Kepler* means hatmaker in German.)

Von Thul's unveiled threats were to prove unavailing since Dodgson's correspondents attest to the fact that he was a stickler for accepting only mail addressed to 'The Rev. C.L. Dodgson, Ch. Ch., Oxford.' Fan mail addressed to Lewis Carroll was either directed to the Dead Letter Office or to Alexander Macmillan, his publisher, but Carrollians should please be aware that the provenance of the aforementioned manuscripts is attributable to neither.

Significantly, in June of 1863, when the events described

occurred, Dodgson's bank overdraft was £148 (the approximate equivalent of £7,500 today).

Anthony Blunt (*In Search of the Fourth Man*)

Blunt's distant 'uncle', the controversial poet and anti-imperialist, Wilfrid Scawen Blunt, was co-founder with his wife of the Crabbet Arabian Stud. A memoir recalling the exploits of the celebrated 'Arab Horsemaster', Farrier-Sergeant George Hugh Lucas Ruxton, president of the Arab Horse Society – in the Somme, Salonica and Palestine – is deposited in the archives of the London Scottish Regiment.

The further trials and tribulations of Josey may be read in Eisner's *Lovesong in Invisible Ink* (pages 6 and 24, *Listen Close to Me*, Salt 2011). Fans of Agatha Christie will be aware that she was a regular guest at Brown's Hotel and wrote a number of her detective novels there.

Constance Bryde (*Inducement*)

For any reader intrigued by the covert activities of PsyOps (operations in psychological warfare, a branch that also embraces, anagrammatically, SpyOps), the episode, *Red Coffee*, in Eisner's *Sister Morphine* (Salt, 2008), describes in some depth the organisational structure of Stoneburgh Military Academy (codenamed 'Oreville'). The reference to 'Ksector-Block8.8g' on Barbara's featurette typescript is explained in the opening passage to *Red Coffee*, in which soldiers at the camp's guardpost view Irina P's arrival with suspicion:

The guards had directed her to 'K' section. The college blocks for the gentlemen cadets and the great park of over six hundred acres had been laid out in tribute to beleaguered forts, border disputes and skirmishes in the Indian and Afghan Wars of the nineteenth century. An entire square mile was divided alphabetically into twenty-six sectors, ranging from Alipur and Berar, through

Charasia to Zulfikar. Irina was detailed to 'K' sector (the siege of Kotah, 1858) which adjoined the Residency of the Lieutenant Governor.

In fact, *Red Coffee*, a spying operation in Central Europe, may be read as the mirror world of Constance's 'blind date' with the secret intelligence community in London, and like Irina, she finds herself enmeshed in undercover activities so convoluted that to separate truth and untruth becomes an impossibility.

Note: The barbiturate derivative drug, Seconal, on which the spy Anthony Blunt depended, calls to mind the fact that the parent-compound for barbiturates was discovered by the great German chemist Adolf von Baeyer on December 4, 1864, the feast of Saint Barbara. How spookily apt, then, that Stoneburgh's SpyOps insider, Barbara Ely, died (in mysterious circumstances) on December 4.

Rhona (*Darkly, More is Seen.*)

Eisner has recorded in a number of texts the debt owed to that great writer of *fin-de-siècle* fiction (and early translator of Freud into English), Ethelind Colburn Mayne. (Mayne's *The Separate Room*, is an ur-text, lest we forget, more than a decade ahead of Woolf's *A Room of One's Own*.) Alert literary sleuth-hounds will undoubtedly draw invidious comparisons between *Darkly* and the autobiographical travails of editorial assistant, Marion, in *The Separate Room* (for her fictive editor, Bergsma, read editor Henry Harland of the *Yellow Book*) whose boss, like Harland, betrays his ghost-writer by supplanting her with one of his favourites. The greatest authority on the life and works of Ethelind Colburn Mayne is the American scholar, Susan Waterman, to whom Eisner is indebted for many fascinating unpublished insights.

By a curious coincidence, the tragedy that befalls Theresa

Ollivante (*A Room to the End of Fall*) has its primal cause in Theresa's Woolfian quest for a 'separate room'.

Anthony Deverell-Hewells (*Now You See It, Now You Don't.*)

The character of this bristling, irrepressible artist, and *camoufleur*, Anthony Deverell-Hewells, is alluded to in a number of Eisner's narratives. The 'Prof' was said to have 'more opinions than the Queen has soldiers.'

And 'the professor's raw complexion rivalled the face of an engineroom stoker . . . and, certainly, "the Prof" never ceased to relish stoking up controversy, for the "rummy old coot" had often claimed he was the first practitioner of Optical Art, and that he had not only invented an invisibility cloak but had caused a battleship to disappear, in a series of trials that had surpassed the Philadelphia Experiment.'

(*Sister Morphine*. Page 312, 344, 346 and 403, *Dispossession* and *A Stranger in Blood*.)

He was a drinking crony of the notorious late British painter, X (German-born). As Grete writes in *Sister Morphine*, see page 133, Deverell-Hewells had evidently learned many of his ruthless womanising stratagems from X, as Grete tells us she had 'learned accidentally from one of X's models that it was the practice of the painter's daughter to issue invitations to the prettier of her girlfriends to meet her celebrated father for lunch, *then not herself show up*. In effect, she was a procuress for her father.'

It should be noted here that Henrietta Goodden's *Camouflage and Art* (2007), in a very real sense, omits a number of the Royal College of Art's alumni who were distinguished serving artists in the camouflage section of the Air Ministry in WW2, whilst only a select rollcall of RCA artists is favoured with inclusion.

Nina (*Private Ledger.*)

As documented on page 41 in the case history, *The Shadow on the Blind* (published in *Listen Close to Me*, 2011), 'Although Neville and Nina were a celebrated couple, they were a team bound together in harness merely by a notional yoke.' This latest instalment of their on-off love affairs refers to a time shortly after their move to Verden Magna when, as Eisner records, 'Nina took a semi-serious long-term lover.'

ACKNOWLEDGEMENTS

Foremost, once again, I would like to express my sincere thanks to the ever vigilant editorial team at Salt for their continuing generous encouragement and guidance in the preparation of this third volume; in particular, Project Editor Jen Hamilton-Emery and – for her creative critique of my sometimes dissentient interpretations of criminal psychopathology – I'd like to specially thank Salt's perceptive Crime Fiction Editor Linda Bennett. I must again praise, too, the consistent support of the staff of that great champion of the experimental arts, the resolutely eclectic literary magazine, *Ambit*, whose founder editor and tireless standard-bearer (in every sense), Dr Martin Bax, has been a guiding influence on the direction of my prose. I am flattered that *Ambit* has regularly published my case studies, and a number of these narratives, in very slightly edited forms, now appear here; our thanks are due to *Ambit* for permission to republish. My thanks also to *Ambit*'s Kate Pemberton, distinguished writer, translator and sensitive editor, whose discerning insights are always enhancers of one's prose; renewed thanks, too, to that eminent Russian translator and protean encyclopedist of Mari El culture, Konstantin Sitnikov, for so generously sharing his knowledge of advances in Chekhovian scholarship, often overlooked in the West; I thank, too, Gordon Dickens of Bulova for so diligently confirming memories of the Bulova factory beneath the Long Island Railroad in Queens, New York; my thanks, too,

to American informants, Sue Brennan of US Postal Operations, Arie Gilbert, the noted ornithologist of Queens County,
Harlan Stone, philatelist, and my special gratitude to William
Ryan, convener of his Golden Anniversary Class Reunion, for
his extraordinary recall of St Teresa School in 'Irishtown' and
that locale's denizens; I am indebted, also, to the University
of Northern Iowa's Professor Roy Behrens, world authority
on the history of camouflage, for his learned commentaries
on military 'countershading'; and, finally, Anthony Blunt's
beskirted skit from the June 1929 issue of *Granta* is repro-
duced with the kind permission of the Syndics of Cambridge
University Library.

Tailpiece

Violante in the pantry,
gnawing of a mutton-bone,
how she gnawed it, how she clawed it,
when she found herself alone.